Naomi had never been kissed until Abe.

And she had never danced with another until tonight.

As he led her onto the dance floor, she didn't care if it was a duty dance, if for one song in her life she was held by him.

But when he held her, when he pulled her into his arms and his hand took hers while the other held her waist, Naomi knew she lied. As she rested her head on his chest, her eyes drifted to the band, and silently pleaded that this dance would never end.

A dangerous mistake.

One only ever read about Abe's scandals.

For all the trysts he'd been caught up in there had never been so much as one single public display of affection.

That ended tonight.

His mouth found hers so easily and both imbibed.

And the band must have sensed her earlier plea for they played on, as the whispers chased the tables around the room.

Abe Devereux and that woman.

Who no one knew by name.

One thing was certain, though, and both tongues and cameras were clicking tonight.

This kiss might have started on the dance floor, but it would end in bed.

Tonight.

Carol Marinelli recently filled in a form asking for her job title. Thrilled to be able to put down her answer, she put "writer." Then it asked what Carol did for relaxation and she put down the truth—"writing." The third question asked for her hobbies. Well, not wanting to look obsessed, she crossed her fingers and answered "swimming"—but, given that the chlorine in the pool does terrible things to her highlights, I'm sure you can guess the real answer!

Books by Carol Marinelli

Harlequin Presents

One Night With Consequences

The Sheikh's Baby Scandal
The Innocent's Shock Pregnancy

Secret Heirs of Billionaires

Claiming His Hidden Heir

Billionaires & One-Night Heirs

The Innocent's Secret Baby
Bound by the Sultan's Baby
Sicilian's Baby of Shame

Ruthless Royal Sheikhs

Captive for the Sheikh's Pleasure

The Billionaire's Legacy

Di Sione's Innocent Conquest

Carol Marinelli

THE BILLIONAIRE'S CHRISTMAS CINDERELLA

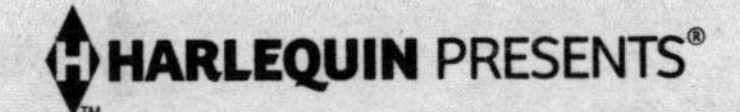

ISBN-13: 978-1-335-41993-4

The Billionaire's Christmas Cinderella

First North American publication 2018

This edition published by arrangement with Harlequin Books S.A.

For questions and comments about the quality of this book, please contact us at CustomerService@Harlequin.com.

Printed in U.S.A.

THE BILLIONAIRE'S CHRISTMAS CINDERELLA

Dear Sam,

With love, always xxxx

PROLOGUE

'I KNOW THAT this is a very difficult time for the Devereux family. However—'

'That may be the case but it has no bearing on this discussion.'

Abe Devereux interrupted the Sheikh when few people would. It was an online meeting, with Abe in his stunning high-rise New York City office and Sheikh Prince Khalid in Al-Kazan, but Abe would have responded in the same terse manner had they met face to face.

The Devereux family was extending its empire into the Middle East. The first hotel was under construction in Dubai and the site for the next had recently been sourced in Al-Kazan.

Except the landowners, Khalid had just informed Abe, had added several million to their previous asking price. To refuse jeopardised not only the Al-Kazan project—the knock-on effect would be huge. If the Devereuxes didn't agree to the new asking price, then construction in Dubai might cease.

Abe refused to be bullied.

Khalid was very possibly relying on the fact that he was a personal friend of Abe's younger brother, Ethan. Or perhaps he had hoped for a rare moment of weakness or distraction, given that Jobe Devereux, the head of the Devereux empire, was gravely ill.

But there would be no weakness or distraction from Abe.

Khalid would soon come to understand that he was dealing with the most ruthless of the Devereuxes.

Abe would never be swayed by emotion.

This was business, and nothing ever got in the way of that.

'Whose side are you on, Khalid?' Abe asked the question few would dare. 'We are supposed to be in this venture together.'

'I am on the side of progress,' Khalid answered smoothly. 'And for the sake of a relatively small sum we risk thwarting the inroads that have been made.'

'If Al-Kazan is not ready for such progress then we shall look for another site.'

'Have you discussed this with Ethan?' Khalid checked.

Ethan was supposed to be here but he hadn't made it in, which was perhaps just as well, given that he was friends with the Sheikh.

Abe wasn't particularly friendly with anyone but, even had he been, it wouldn't have swayed him.

'Ethan and I are both in full agreement,' Abe lied smoothly, for he had not had a chance to speak with his brother. 'The price remains as originally decided or we look elsewhere.'

'If we could perhaps discuss it with Ethan present?' Supremely polite, still Khalid pushed his agenda. 'He was here recently and understands the sensitivities.'

'There's nothing more to discuss.'

'But if we can't come to a satisfactory resolution, even a temporary one, construction in Dubai may well cease.'

'In that case…' Abe shrugged '…no one gets paid. Now, if you'll excuse me, I really do have to go.'

'Of course.' Khalid nodded graciously, though it was clear he was displeased. 'Would you pass on my best wishes to your father?'

It was only when Abe was satisfied that they had been disconnected and Khalid's face had disappeared from the screen that he let out a curse that indicated the gravity of the situation. If the Dubai construction ceased, for even a few days, the knock-on effect would be dire.

Abe was quite sure that Khalid was relying on that fact.

For a couple of million, Abe could resolve this. It was small change in the scheme of things and he was certain that Ethan would be willing to pay up rather than jeopardise the project at this tender stage.

But Abe refused to be bullied.

And threats, however silkily delivered, would not change his stance.

Abe got up from his desk and, from his impressive vantage point, looked out over a cold and snowy Manhattan and beyond. It was a stunning view towards the East River and he drank it in for a moment, barely turning his head when his brother's PA knocked and explained the reason for his absence from this morning's meeting.

'Ethan's been at the hospital with Merida since last night. Apparently, she's in labour.'

'Thank you.'

Abe didn't ask for details.

He already knew more than enough.

Ethan had married Merida a few months ago, though only because she was pregnant. Abe had, along with his father, signed off on the contract that would ensure that the new Mrs Devereux and her infant would be well provided for when they eventually divorced.

But as clinical as a contract sounded, it had its merits—Abe hoped to God it ensured that the baby would be treated better than he and Ethan had been.

He could not think of that now.

Abe closed his eyes on the glorious December view.

It wasn't even nine a.m. and it was already proving to be a long day.

He had Sheikh Khalid testing his limits and the Middle East contract on the brink of collapse.

As well as that, in the hospital a few streets away from this very building he had his brother's wife giving birth in one wing…

And his father dying in the other.

No.

He corrected himself—his father was fighting for his life in the other.

His mother, Elizabeth Devereux, had died when Abe was nine. She hadn't been in the least bit maternal and Jobe had been far from a hands-on father. In fact, a fleet of nannies had raised the Devereux boys—but Abe greatly admired his father and was not ready to let him go.

Not that he showed it, of course.

For a second so brief it was barely there Abe considered discussing the Middle East issue with him. Jobe Devereux was the founder and the cleverest man Abe knew. Yet Abe quickly decided he could not stress his father while he was fighting just to survive.

Only that wasn't the real reason that Abe didn't head to the hospital now—Jobe had never shied from giving his view after all.

It was more that Abe had never asked for help in his life.

And he wasn't about to start now.

But before he could tackle the work waiting,

his private phone rang and Abe saw that it was his brother.

'A little girl,' Ethan said, sounding both tired and elated at the same time.

'Congratulations.'

'Merida was amazing!'

Abe made no comment to that. The fact that Merida had just had a baby did not suddenly make him a fan of hers. 'Have you told Dad?'

'I'm heading over to tell him now,' Ethan said.

Usually they called their father Jobe, as it helped with the business side of things, but this, Abe was fast realising, wasn't business.

Oh, there might be a watertight contract in place and the marriage might all be a charade, but a little girl had been born this morning. And that moved him. He thought of his father, about to hear the news that he was a grandfather.

'Will you be coming in to meet your niece?' Ethan asked.

'Of course.' Abe glanced at the time. 'Though not until later in the afternoon.'

'Merida's friend, Naomi, is getting in at midday. We were supposed to be there to meet her.'

'Do you want me to organise a driver to pick her up?'

There was a brief stretch of silence before Ethan responded. Neither of the brothers liked asking for help, even from the other. 'Abe, is there any chance of you going? She's Merida's best friend.'

'I thought she was the nanny?' Abe frowned. He only knew that because a full-time live-in nanny had been a part of the terms agreed to.

'Naomi's both.'

'Give me her details,' Abe sighed, and pulled out a pen.

'Naomi Hamilton.' Ethan gave her flight details. 'If she can come to the hospital before being taken to the house, that would be good.'

'All sorted,' Abe said, and glanced again at the time. 'I really do have to go. Congratulations.'

'Thanks.'

Luckily Ethan was too muddled to ask how this morning's meeting with Khalid had gone and certainly Abe did not volunteer the information.

Cool heads were needed for dealing with this situation and currently the only Devereux who had one was Abe.

He buzzed through to his own PA. 'Jessica, could you organise a gift for me to take to the hospital this afternoon?'

'For your father?' she checked.

'No, the baby's here.'

There was a little squeal that had Abe pulling the phone back from his ear; then came the inevitable questions. 'What did Merida have?'

'A girl.'

'Does she have a name yet? Do you know how much she weighs?'

'I don't know any more than that,' Abe responded. He really hadn't thought to ask. 'I also need you to sort out a driver to do an airport run from JFK to the hospital.' He gave the flight details. 'She gets in at midday. The name's Naomi Hamilton.'

Despite his brother's request, Abe would *not* be playing chauffeur.

As well as Khalid to contend with, he had the first-of-the-month board meeting to attend. Before that he was meeting with Maurice, the head of PR, to discuss the annual Devereux Christmas Eve Charity Ball.

It was a highlight on the social calendar, but, for the first time since its inception, Jobe Devereux would not be attending.

Tabled on this morning's agenda was discussion of contingency plans should Jobe die close to, or on, that date.

Not pleasant.

But a necessary task, given that people travelled from far and wide and paid an awful lot of money to attend.

Emotion had to be put aside and unpalatable scenarios played out and usually Abe was very good at that.

Abe wasn't just cool…he was considered cold.

And not just in the boardroom. His reputation

with women was devastating, though that had calmed in recent years. But his aloofness extended also to family.

He had stopped trusting others by the age of four, looking out for his brother and doing his best to ensure that he came to no harm.

Abe kept his emotions in check.

Yet, unusually, this morning he was struggling to do that.

His schedule was always daunting but he thrived on the pressure and handled it with ease. Yet the autopilot he usually ran on felt, this morning, as if it had disengaged.

The news of the baby had punched a hole in the wall he carefully erected between himself and others.

He put a finger and thumb to the bridge of his nose and squeezed hard, then took a long cleansing breath. Pushing all the drama out of his mind, he'd get on with holding down the Devereux fort.

Someone had to.

CHAPTER ONE

'A NEW YORK CHRISTMAS...'

Naomi smiled as her very chatty fellow passenger told her what a magical time she would soon be having.

'There's nothing better.'

'I'm sure there isn't,' Naomi agreed.

It was easier to.

Privately she cared little for the festive season. Well, she made sure it all went smoothly for whatever family she was with but it was just another day for Naomi.

Actually, no. It was a very lonely day for Naomi—it always had been and no doubt always would be.

But she wasn't going to bore the woman in the next seat with that.

They had got on well.

Naomi was a little on the large side and had tucked her elbows in and tried to make herself very small on take-off. But by the time they came into land, neither had slept and they were chatting away like old friends. Still, there were things even old friends didn't need to know.

Born on Christmas Eve, from the little Naomi knew her first weeks of life had been spent on a maternity ward before the first of many foster-care placements.

Now a maternity nanny, she looked after newborns and ensured better for her tiny charges. Her job was to look after the mother and infant during this very precious, tumultuous time before the permanent nanny took over.

She wasn't a part of the family, though.

On a day such as Christmas, her role was to make it as seamless and as stress-free for the new mother as possible. And Naomi usually ate in her room alone.

This year, though, would be different as it was her best friend whose baby she would be taking care of.

Merida, an actress, had come to New York City with Broadway on her mind and, sure enough, had landed a part in a new production called *Night Forest*.

She had never made it to opening night, though.

Pregnant by Ethan Devereux, she had said goodbye to her acting career and entered into a marriage of convenience.

Although, inconveniently for Merida, she was head over heels in love with her husband.

Naomi had had reservations about accepting the job.

Ethan and Merida had insisted that she be paid, and though they were probably just trying to be nice, it would have been easier on Naomi to have been asked to stay as a friend.

But she was concerned for Merida and that was why she had agreed to take the post.

As the cabin lights were dimmed for landing, Naomi looked out of the small, moisture-streaked window. There wasn't much to see, just snow-laden clouds, but then her breath caught as jutting up in the distance she saw the iconic skyline rising out from gunmetal-grey water and it sent a frisson of excitement through Naomi. She was here—actually here. And for someone who had never been out of the United Kingdom it was an exciting moment indeed.

The plane banked for its final approach but that first glimpse of the city left a smile on Naomi's face.

Naomi had freshened up as best she could after breakfast had been served but she took out her compact and checked her reflection. She was excited to see Merida but her reflection showed tiredness. Her dark chocolate curls were limp and beneath her deep blue eyes were dark smudges. Her very pale complexion had turned to pure white.

A sleep would fix that, she told herself.

Naomi was determined to beat jet lag at its own game and stay awake for the entire day.

It was beyond exciting to be here and she wore her smile through baggage collection, though she felt it wane a touch at customs.

All the paperwork had been arranged but still she felt very nervous when she told them that, yes, she was here to work.

'A nanny?' the border security official checked, and took the folder containing all of Naomi's paperwork and had a through read through of it. 'For the Devereuxes?'

'Yes, there's a letter from Mr Ethan Devereux and if there are any problems…'

'There's no problem.'

Her passport was stamped and she was on her way.

The ground staff were lively and funny, blowing into their hands and telling her it was bitterly cold as she awaited her baggage.

'You'll need a coat, Miss,' one said as she passed.

'I'm getting one!' Naomi called back. 'I'm headed straight to the shops.'

She had, a few days previously, left her good coat on a train and had been about to buy one for her trip when it had dawned on her she was heading to the shopping capital of the world. Naomi had decided her first stop would be the city's most famous department store.

For now she had to make do with a rather flimsy

jacket and a thick scarf that she would put over her long dark hair before heading outside.

Naomi had a lot of luggage.

Well, two cases and her hand luggage.

It was, though, her entire world that she carried in those bags.

She lived wherever work took her. In between jobs she aimed to take a brief holiday, but Naomi didn't have a home as such. She had shared a flat with Merida for a couple of years, which had been brilliant, but since then she had lived with the families she'd cared for. Generally, she arrived two weeks before the baby's due date and stayed between six and eight weeks after the baby was born.

And she was tired of it.

Not so much her work, as exhausting as it was.

Naomi was just tired of living out of suitcases.

As she stepped into the arrivals lounge Naomi scanned the crowd for a glimpse of Merida, who was generally unmissable with her shock of red hair, although, given how cold it was, she may well be wearing a hat. Or, given that the baby was due on December the fourteenth, she may well have not made it to the airport. As she wheeled her trolley Merida saw a sign with her name on it held by an older man in a black suit.

'I'm Naomi Hamilton,' she said.

'Guest of?' the gentleman asked.

Clearly security was tight around the family,

Naomi thought as her status was double checked. 'Merida Devereux.'

'Then come this way.' He smiled. 'Here, let me help you with that…' He took over the trolley. 'Where's your coat?'

Naomi told him her plan to get one as they walked and it really was freezing outside.

'Jump in,' he told her when they reached the car. Naomi didn't need to be asked twice and sat in the back, watching the world go by as her cases were loaded.

'Are we headed to the house?' Naomi asked as they drove off.

'No.' He gave her a smile in the rear-view mirror. 'I'm to take you to the hospital. More than that, I don't know.'

How exciting!

Naomi was very aware, though, that the next few weeks were not going to be plain sailing. Merida was completely in love with Ethan, who had only married her to give the child his name, and the plan was they would divorce after a year. Naomi was worried for Merida. Also, the patriarch of the family, Jobe Devereux, was seriously ill.

Even if Merida hadn't been her friend, Naomi would have been aware of that fact. The Devereuxes were a hugely powerful family and Jobe's health woes had reached the press in England.

Naomi just wanted to make these precious first

weeks as peaceful and as calm as she could for the new mother and baby, and would do whatever she could to ensure that.

The car was warm and despite the stop-start traffic it was lulling, and as they drove through a long tunnel Naomi resisted the urge to rest her head on the window and close her eyes. But, given she'd had to be at Heathrow so early, she hadn't slept last night, neither had she slept on the plane, and as the traffic backed up Naomi found that her eyelids grew heavy and finally she gave in.

'Miss...'

Naomi startled and opened her eyes, taking a second to gather where she was. In fact, the driver had to orientate her.

'We're at the hospital.'

So they were.

The private wing was incredibly warm and as she passed a couple of rooms and saw empty beds Naomi thought about how she would love to claim one and stretch out and sleep; but as she stepped into Merida's room jet lag was completely forgotten.

'Naomi!' Merida was sitting up in bed, looking a mixture of exhausted and happy and clearly delighted by the arrival of her friend.

'Merida! How are you?'

'So happy. We had a girl.'

Ethan was holding the precious bundle. 'I'm sorry I couldn't get there to meet you,' he said, giving her a kiss on the cheek, and was rather more friendly than Naomi had expected.

'Well, you were rather busy...' Naomi smiled.

'Is Abe with you?' he asked.

'Abe?' Naomi frowned for a second then remembered that was Abe was the elder Devereux brother. 'No, the driver brought me. Bernard, I think...' She was distracted then as the blanket fell back and she caught a proper glimpse of the baby. 'Oh, my, she is gorgeous.'

Naomi, in her line of work, saw a lot of new babies, and they were all very precious, though for Naomi there had never been one more precious than this little girl. With no relatives of her own, Merida and her very new daughter were the closest thing to family that Naomi had known.

When Ethan handed her to Naomi she found that her eyes filled up with tears as she held the new life.

'Does she have a name?'

'Ava,' Merida said. 'We just decided.'

'Oh, but it suits her. She's completely stunning.' Little Ava really was, with a shock of dark hair like her father, and huge dark blue eyes and a sweet little rosebud mouth. 'How was the birth?'

'It was actually wonderful.'

When Ethan headed off to make some calls, Merida elaborated a touch. 'Ethan was right there the whole time. Naomi, we're okay now,' Merida said, her eyes shining. 'Ethan told me he loves me and that we're going to make this marriage work.'

Naomi rather thought it might be the emotion of the birth that had Ethan showing devotion, but of course she didn't say that to her friend as she popped the now sleeping baby into her little crib.

'How long do you think you'll be in for?' Naomi asked.

'A couple of days. I feel terrible that you'll have to find your own way around.'

'I'm quite sure I can manage. I'll head off soon and get in some sleep and tomorrow I might do a bit of sightseeing *and* buy a decent coat.'

'I can't believe you're actually here.' Merida beamed. 'Naomi, I've got so much to tell you.'

But it would all have to wait.

Ethan returned at that moment and a short while later Jobe, the grandfather of little Ava, came down in a wheelchair, escorted by a nurse. And then came the photos, though not just the family kind—a professional photographer had been brought in for the occasion.

It was clear that Jobe was very ill indeed, yet he had refused to have the baby brought up to visit him and had made a supreme effort to be a part of such an important day.

As the photographer snapped away, even though Jobe had a nurse with him, Naomi helped too, positioning little Ava in his arms and making sure that as soon as he tired she took the baby with a smile.

'Thank you,' Jobe said, noting how she had hovered discreetly. 'You're Merida's friend?'

'Yes.' Naomi nodded. 'And also little Ava's nanny for the next few weeks.'

'Well, any friend of Merida's is a friend of the family. It's good to have you here, Naomi.'

It was such a little thing. She had expected to be daunted by this powerful man, but instead they clicked on sight and he made Naomi feel very welcome and a part of it all. She was used to being the nanny and hovering in the background, but today, on her first day in New York, she'd had her picture taken while holding a tiny little baby who was new to all of this too!

'Has Abe been in?' Jobe asked, as Naomi held little Ava, who was close to falling asleep in her arms.

Naomi might look as if she wasn't listening, but her ears were on elastic. She knew Abe was a force to be reckoned with and wanted to get a feel for things and work out the dynamics so that she could help Merida as best she could in the weeks ahead.

'Not as yet,' Ethan said, and Naomi heard the edge to his voice. 'I specifically asked him to pick up Naomi, but instead he sent a car.'

'Well, he must have got caught up,' Jobe suggested.

With little Ava asleep and Merida looking like she needed the same, Naomi decided it was time to head off. 'I'm going to go,' she said, and gave Merida a hug and a kiss. 'Jet lag is starting to creep in and I want that well behind me by the time you bring your little lady home.'

'We're staying at Dad's place for now,' Ethan explained, 'while we have some renovations done.'

'Merida told me.' Naomi nodded. 'It's fine.'

Famous last words.

'Dad's place' was a huge, grey stone mansion on Fifth Avenue, overlooking Central Park. Naomi had to pinch herself to believe that she was really here. Oh, thanks to her job she had stayed in some amazing residences, but nowhere had been nearly as grand as this.

One of the heavy double doors was opened by a gentleman who said that they had been expecting her, and as Naomi stepped into the foyer an elderly woman came rushing over.

'Naomi!' She gave her a welcoming smile. 'I'm Barb, Head of Housekeeping.'

'It's lovely to meet you, Barb.'

The house was even more stunning inside.

The huge foyer with marble floors and archways was impressive, as was the large curved staircase, but it was all made a little less daunting because the first thing that greeted Naomi was the delicious scent of pine.

There in the corner was a Christmas tree, bigger than any she had ever seen.

An undressed tree.

'We were waiting to find out what Merida had,' Barb explained. 'Have you ever seen a tree decorated pink?'

'No.' Naomi laughed.

'Well, you soon will.'

And even with a soon-to-be-pink tree it was sheer New York elegance and this was only the entrance. Naomi could only imagine what lay behind the high doors.

'Have you seen the baby?' Barb asked.

'Yes, she's very beautiful. She's got black hair and a lot of it…'

'Oh, how precious.'

Naomi didn't reveal her name, or show the photos she had taken with her phone, as she wasn't sure it was her place to. Not that Barb asked, she was far too busy chatting. 'It's fantastic that you've arrived on such a good news day. We were just having a little celebration,' she added. 'I'll show you around.'

'That can wait.' Naomi shook her head. 'A bath and bed is all I need right now. Just show me where I'm sleeping and you can get back to celebrating the baby's arrival. Though if you can show me the alarm system, that would be great. I don't want to set it off if I get up in the night.'

Barb did so and as they walked up a huge staircase, lined with family photos Naomi told her about the time she'd had to call an ambulance on her first night at a job for the mother of one of her charges. 'When I let the paramedics in I set the whole house off. It just added to the chaos.'

'What a fright you must have had,' Barb said as she huffed up the stairs. 'Now, don't turn left here or you'll end up in Abe's wing.'

'Does he live here?' Naomi asked, because she hadn't been expecting that, but Barb shook her head.

'No, he's half an hour away, but if he's been visiting his father late into the night, sometimes he comes home.' She gave a little laugh. 'Well, to the family home. Now, this is you.'

She opened a heavy door, and behind it wasn't the bedroom that Naomi had been expecting to see. Instead, it was more of an apartment, with a lounge, its own bathroom, a small kitchen as well as a bedroom. 'And the baby has a room, of course…' Barb said, opening the door onto a small nursery. It wasn't the main one—this nursery was, Naomi rightly guessed, for the times the nanny had the baby overnight. Not that Merida was intending for that to happen, she had made it clear she wanted the baby with her, but it gave Naomi a glimpse of how things had once worked in the Devereux home.

'I have to say, I never thought I'd see the day when we had a nanny here again,' Barb admitted. 'I got on well with the last one.'

'How long ago was that?'

'Let me see, Abe must be nearly thirty-five and

Ethan's thirty. They had nannies till they went off to boarding school, so Ethan's last one must have been some twenty years ago. They had their work cut out, let me tell you…' Barb's flow of words halted.

'Did the boys run wild?' Naomi pried, but Barb changed the subject.

'Now, Merida made it very clear that you're a guest as well as the baby's nanny, so you're to use the main entrance, as well as having access to a driver, and you've got full freedom of the house. Still, it might be nice for you to have your own space.'

Naomi nodded.

She guessed that Barb had stopped talking so freely when she'd remembered that Naomi wasn't just staff but also a guest.

'I'll bring you up some dinner, or you're more than welcome to join us. We're just having some nibbles…'

'Don't worry about dinner for me.' Naomi shook her head. 'I ate on the plane. All I want now is a bath and then bed.'

'Well, you make sure to let me know if you wake up hungry.'

'If I do, I'll call out for something,' Naomi said. She was very used to staying in new places. 'You go and celebrate and don't worry about me.'

Once Barb had gone Naomi explored a little. Her bedroom was gorgeous, dressed in lemon and cream with a splash of willow green, and Naomi couldn't wait to crawl into the plump bed, but first she unpacked and then had a long bath. She had intended it to be a quick one but she dozed off in the middle. She really was very tired so pulled on some pyjamas and crawled into bed. It was delicious to stretch out but sleep wasn't as forthcoming as she'd hoped it would be, and she lay there with her mind whirring.

A little girl.

Ava.

Oh, she was so thrilled for Merida but, despite her friend's assurances that everything was fine now, Naomi was very aware that that might just be the high of giving birth and Ethan making promises he might not keep.

Yes, he'd seemed friendly and happy but the Devereuxes were not exactly famous for their devotion to their marriage vows.

Naomi was also worried about the dark times ahead because, having seen Jobe, it was clear to her that he was nearing the end.

It was certainly going to be an emotional time and Naomi was glad that she would be here for her friend.

Ava hadn't been due for another two weeks. Naomi's loose plan had been to get over jet lag, as well as the exhaustion of her previous job—usually she would have allowed for more time between jobs but for Merida she had made an exception.

Really, she didn't consider Merida work, though they had insisted on paying her handsomely.

It still didn't sit quite right with Naomi, but she tried not to think of that now.

Her plan had been to catch up on her sleep and get her bearings, and to do some sightseeing at the start of her trip. With Ava's slightly early arrival all her plans had changed.

Tomorrow, she decided, she would go through the nursery and check if there was anything needed and then she'd call the hospital. And then she'd cram in as much sightseeing as possible. Before she could do that, though, she had to buy a coat.

It was on that thought that she fell asleep and then awoke, Naomi had no idea how much time later, to the unsettling feeling she generally had during her first couple of days in a new home.

There was an eerie silence.

Soon she would wake knowing where she was and recognising the shadows on the walls, Naomi told herself as she lay there, but for now it was all unfamiliar.

One feeling she did recognise, though, was the fact that she was starving.

Usually she would have emergency supplies for nights such as this, but there was nothing in her luggage, and anyway a snack wasn't going to fix this hunger.

Naomi pulled on her robe and drew back the drapes, then understood the odd silence for there was a blanket of snow outside and it was still falling heavily.

Even though the house was warm, the sight made her shiver and she did up the ties on her robe.

It was coming up for midnight and, Naomi decided, there was just one thing she wanted more than anything in the world on her first night in New York.

Pizza.

A big pepperoni pizza, but she wondered if they'd deliver.

No problem!

Naomi ordered online and just fifteen minutes later tracked her pizza working its way along Fifth Avenue!

She padded down the stairs and was just about to sort the alarm when she startled as the front doors opened. A dark-coated man walked through them, bringing with him a blast of cold air and, to Naomi, the warmest of glows.

Perhaps he floated through them, Naomi thought, for he was almost too beautiful to be mortal.

He was *more*.

It was the only word she could come up with as she stood in the grand entrance, yet it was an apt one.

He was a smidge taller than Ethan and his jet-black hair was worn a touch longer, and was currently flecked with snow. And he was more sullen in appearance than his brother had been, with almost accusing black eyes narrowing as they met hers.

And he was, to Naomi, a whole lot sexier.

Yes, he was *more*.

He made her heart quicken and she was suddenly terribly aware of her night attire and tangle of hair, because he was just so groomed and glossy and more beautiful than anyone she had ever seen.

'I thought not,' Naomi said by way of greeting.

And Abe frowned because not only did he have no idea what she meant, he also had no idea who this voluptuous dark-haired beauty, dressed in her nightwear, was.

Then she walked past him and he watched as she took delivery of a large pizza box and now he better understood her odd greeting.

No, Abe Devereux was definitely not the pizza delivery man!

CHAPTER TWO

'I'M NAOMI,' SHE offered by way of introduction as she closed the front door. 'Merida's friend and the baby's nanny.'

'Abe,' he said, but didn't elaborate. It was his father's home after all and he was also in no mood to engage in small talk.

But she persisted.

'Have you seen her?' Naomi asked. 'The baby.'

'Yes.'

He said no more than that. Abe Devereux did not offer his thoughts or his opinions. There was no 'Yes, isn't she gorgeous!' No 'I can't believe I'm an uncle,' and it was clear to Naomi that he did not want to speak.

It didn't offend her.

Naomi was *very* used to being the paid staff.

He removed an elegant grey woollen coat and beneath that was a suit, cut to perfection, enhancing his tall, lean frame.

Abe glanced briefly around, no doubt, Naomi

thought, expecting someone to come and take his coat, but when no one appeared, neither did Naomi hold out her hand. With that lack of a gesture she drew a very important line. She might be staff, but she was Ava's nanny, and *not* his maid.

He tossed the coat over an occasional chair as Naomi opened the lid of her pizza box and peered into it. 'I'll say goodnight…' She was momentarily distracted from his utter, imposing beauty by the sight that greeted her. 'Just how big is this thing?' Naomi asked.

The pizza was massive.

Seriously so.

It smelt utterly divine.

And, she remembered, she was not just the nanny but Merida's friend, and so she persisted with the conversation when perhaps usually she would not.

'Would you like some?' she offered, but Abe didn't even bother to reply so she took her cue and headed up the stairs.

There were pictures lining the walls of the stunning Devereux family over the years. The two brothers, as babies and then children. Their stunning mother who, Naomi knew, was dead. She wondered if they missed her on a day like today.

Yes, Naomi often wondered about things like this, especially with not having a family of her own.

And then she heard his voice.

'I would.'

She turned on the stairs, a little unsure what he meant. Did Abe Devereux actually want to share in her midnight feast, or had she got things completely wrong and he was about to tell her he would like staff to refrain from wandering at night, or something?

But, no, she hadn't got things wrong.

'A slice of pizza sounds good,' Abe confirmed.

He himself was surprised that he had taken her up on her offer. And it wasn't the normality of it that had had him say yes, for it was far from normal—Abe didn't do pizza. And, more pointedly, a woman in pale pink pyjamas with a big robe on top wasn't the norm either. Silk or skin was the usual sight that greeted him at this time of night.

He had just come from the hospital, though not the maternity section for he had visited his brother and wife earlier in the day.

Instead, he had spent the evening and half the night with his father.

Jobe had put everything into staying alive for the baby's birth and visiting the little family today, and Abe had this terrible, awful feeling that now it was done he'd just fade.

He had sat there, watching his father sleep and the snow floating past the window, and though warm in the hospital room he had felt chilled to the bone.

They might not be particularly close but Abe admired his father more than anyone in the world.

Ethan had grown up never knowing what a cruel woman their mother had been.

Four years older than his brother, Abe had known.

Elizabeth Devereux's death when he was nine had come as a shock, but all these years later Abe already grieved for his father.

Not that he showed it.

Abe had long since closed off his heart and far from hiding his emotions, he *chose* not to feel them.

Yet choice had been unavailable to him tonight.

'Why couldn't you come to me, Abe?' his father had asked, when his medication had been given for the night.

'It will sort itself out,' Abe had said. 'Khalid is just posturing.'

'I'm not talking about Khalid,' Jobe had snapped, and then, defeated by the drugs, had closed his eyes to sleep.

Yet where was the peace? Abe thought, for despite the good news of the day, despite Jobe's goal to see his grandchild being met, still his face was lined and there was tension visible even in his drug-induced sleep.

There had been a long moment when his father's breathing had seemed to cease and he'd called urgently for the nurse.

It was normal, he'd been told, with so much morphine for respirations to decrease and also, he'd been further told, albeit gently, things slowed down near the end of life.

But no matter how gently said, it had hit him like a fist to the gut.

His father was dying.

Oh, he had known for months, of course he had, but he had fully realised it then. Abe had glimpsed the utter finality of what was to come and, rather than do what instinct told him to and shake his father awake and demand that he not die, Abe had held it in and headed out into the snowy night.

He had sent his driver home ages ago, and had stood for a moment looking up at the snow falling so quietly from the sky.

Instead of calling for his driver, or even hailing a cab, he had crossed the wide street and headed over to Central Park.

There he had cleared snow from a bench and sat by the reservoir, too numb, and grateful for that fact, to feel the cold.

Here had been the park of his childhood, though it had never been a playground.

Abe had never played.

Instead, on the occasional times his mother would take them, unaccompanied by a nanny, it would be he who would look out for Ethan, making sure he didn't get too close to the water.

And that had been on a good day.

The park closed at one a.m. and, rather than being

locked in for the night, Abe had stood with no intention of heading home.

There were plenty he could call upon for the usual balm of sex. As disengaged as he was with his lovers, Abe did generally at least manage some conversation, but even that brief overture before the mind-numbing act felt like too much effort tonight.

And so he had walked from the park to his father's residence, which was far closer to the hospital than his Greenwich Village home. He had decided to sleep there tonight.

Just in case.

And now, for reasons he didn't care to examine, conversation felt welcome.

Necessary even.

He walked through to the drawing room and she, Naomi, Merida's friend, followed him in and took a seat on the pale blue sofa as he lit the fire that had been made up and then checked his phone.

Again, just in case.

'The snow's getting heavy,' he said. 'I thought it might be wise to stay nearer to the hospital tonight.'

'How is your father?'

'Today took a lot out of him. Are you a nurse?' he asked, because he had no real idea of the qualifications required to be a nanny. Perhaps that was why he had pursued conversation, Abe thought—so that he could pick her brains.

But she shook her head.

'No,' Naomi said. 'I'd always wanted to be a paediatric nurse but…' She gave an uncomfortable shrug. 'It didn't work out.'

'Why not?'

'I didn't do too well at school.'

She opened up the box again and tore off one of the large slices but the topping slid off as she attempted to raise it to her mouth. 'How on earth do you eat this?'

'Not like that,' he said, and he showed her how to fold the huge triangle.

'I haven't had pizza from a box in years…' Abe mused as he took his slice. 'Or rather decades. Jobe used to take Ethan and me over to Brooklyn when we were small. We'd sit on the pier…' His voice trailed off and he was incredibly grateful that she didn't fill the silence that followed so he could just sit and hold the memory for a moment as they ate quietly. 'This pizza's good,' he commented.

'It's better than good, it's incredible.' And made more so when he went and poured two generous drinks from a decanter.

'Cognac?' he offered.

She had never tasted it before and, given for once she wasn't working, Naomi took the glass when he handed it to her.

'Wow,' she said, because it burnt as it went down. 'I doubt I'll have much trouble getting back to sleep after that.'

'That's the aim,' Abe said. 'You can rely on my father to have the good stuff on tap.'

'What did you think of the baby?' Naomi asked as he sat down. Not on the sofa but on the floor, leaning against it.

'It's very loud,' Abe said, and she laughed.

'She's gorgeous. What are you getting her as a gift?'

'Already done.' Abe yawned before continuing. 'My PA dealt with it and got her some silver teddy.'

'I did all the shopping before I came,' Naomi said, 'though now I know it's a girl I'm sure there'll be more. Are you excited to be an uncle?'

He raised his eyes, somewhat disarmed by her question.

Abe really hadn't given being an uncle much thought. Since he'd heard that his brother had got Merida pregnant it had been the legalities that he'd focussed on—making sure the baby was a US citizen and ensuring Merida couldn't get her hands on any more of the Devereux fortune than the baby assured her.

Only, lately, Merida seemed less and less like the woman Abe had been so certain she was.

In fact, Ethan looked happy.

He didn't say any of that, of course.

But if you are going to do pizza by the fire on a snowy December night, you do need to do your share of talking, and so he asked her a question. 'Do you have any nieces or nephews?'

'No.' Naomi shook her head and then let out a dreamy sigh. 'I actually can't think of anything nicer than to be an aunt.'

'Do you have any brothers or sisters who might one day oblige you?'

She shook her head.

'So you're an only child?' he casually assumed, and then watched as for the first time colour came to her pale cheeks.

'I don't have any family.'

He saw the slight tremble of her fingers as she put down the crust of her pizza.

'None?' he checked.

'I count Merida as family,' she admitted, 'but, no.'

Yes, she and Merida were close, but Naomi was very aware that though they were best friends, Merida was far more of Naomi's world than the other way around.

And that said nothing against Merida. But she had parents, albeit awful ones, and a half-brother and half-sister, and cousins and grandparents.

Naomi had…

Merida.

Her birth mother had wanted nothing whatsoever to do with her and Naomi had no clue who her father was. There had been a foster mum when she'd been a teenager that had been amazing but she'd taken a well-earned retirement in Spain, though they still corresponded. And there was another foster family that she still sent a Christmas card to.

And of course, there were friends she had made along life's way, but there was no family.

None.

Zip.

'My mother gave me up for adoption,' Naomi said, 'but it never happened.'

She tensed as she awaited the inevitable 'Why?' that even virtual strangers felt compelled to ask.

It just made her feel worse.

There were millions of families who wanted babies, surely?

Or, 'What about your grandparents, didn't they want you?'

It was hell having to explain that, no, her mother hadn't fully relinquished her rights for a few years, which had held Naomi in the foster system. And, no, her grandparents hadn't wanted to clear up their daughter's mess.

And that, no, there would be no tender reunion between mother and daughter.

At the age of eighteen Naomi had tried.

But her mother had remarried and wanted no reminder of her rebellious past.

Thankfully, though, Abe didn't ask.

Instead, he watched her pinched face and two lines deepen between her dark blue eyes like a castle gate drawing up in defence. He thought of his own loud, brash family and the dramas and fights at times. He even thought back to his mother, and while there were no warm memories there, still there was history.

He couldn't fathom having no one.

Yet he did not pry.

And she seemed incredibly grateful for that.

He watched as she visibly shook off dark thoughts and pushed out a smile.

'So what sort of an uncle do you want to be?' Naomi asked.

Given what she'd just told him, he didn't dust off the notion, instead he told her the truth. 'I really haven't given it much thought.' Now he did. 'I don't know,' he admitted. 'I can't imagine that she'd want for anything...' He'd made very sure of that. But as he'd combed through the contract and ensured decent chunks of access for his brother, there had been no thought of where he himself might fit in.

'I'd like to be...' Who examined it? Abe wondered. Who actually gave consideration to the type of uncle they wanted to be?

She had made him do just that.

He could hear the spit and crackle of the fire as he gazed into it. Maybe he was feeling maudlin. It would be his father's funeral soon after all, but on this cold December night, the most guarded and closed off of all the Devereuxes paused a while and thought of the uncle he would like to be.

'I could take her for pizza now and then,' he said.

'And show her how to eat it?'

'Yes,' he agreed, but then shook his head. 'I can't think of anything else.'

'That's plenty to be going on with.' Naomi smiled and when he tore off another slice, it seemed easier, rather than have him hand it to her, to join him on the floor. It simply did. And they sat side by side and spoke, not a lot but enough.

'So,' he asked, 'you're going to be looking after Ava?'

'For a little while.' She saw his frown. 'I'm a maternity nanny.'

'What does that mean?'

'I generally stay between six and eight weeks with a new family before the permanent nanny takes over. I try to allocate four weeks between jobs, but it never really works out. Babies come early, as we saw today.'

'Do you go home between jobs?'

'No, I generally have a holiday. Sometimes if there's a decent gap I might house-sit.'

'Where's home?'

'The next job.'

'So you're a nomadic nanny.'

'I guess.' That made her laugh, she'd never really thought of describing it like that. 'Yes.'

'And you only look after newborns?'

She nodded.

'That sounds like constant hard work.'

'Oh, it is,' Naomi agreed. 'But I completely love it.'

Or she had.

Naomi didn't share that with him, of course. She didn't tell him that she was tired in a way she'd never been before. Not just from lack of sleep but from the constant motion of her lifestyle.

There was one slice of pizza left and both their hands reached for it at the same time.

'Go ahead,' Abe said.

'No, we'll share it.'

And when he tore it and there was one half a bit bigger, instead of not noticing, she looked at him until he tore a piece off the bigger half. 'That's fair now,' Abe said.

'Hmm.'

She was so full it shouldn't matter, but she had never, ever tasted something so delicious, Naomi thought. Or was it the open fire keeping them warm as the snow fluttered outside the window, or was it adult company in the middle of the night that made it all so nice?

'Do you ever have,' Abe asked, 'er, *issues* with the fathers?'

'Gosh no.' Naomi laughed. 'I dress like this for work. I don't think the mothers have anything to worry about.'

He begged to differ.

Scantily dressed Naomi wasn't, but for Ethan there was no doubting her sensuality. It wasn't just her curves or the very full mouth or ripple of dark hair and how it fell in her eyes, it was more subtle than that. Little things, like the way she covered herself when her robe gaped, and how she closed her eyes after each and every sip of cognac as she held it on her tongue for a moment, and the lick of her lips when she'd first glimpsed the pizza.

Yet, he mused, the mothers wouldn't have anything to worry about.

She was nice.

Moral.

The sort you would trust your baby to.

And for Abe she had made this hellish night so much better.

'Do you ever get asked to stay on?' Abe asked.

'All the time.' Naomi nodded and then took the last bit of her pizza and he waited, watching the column of her pale throat as she swallowed, before asking another question.

'And do you ever consider it?'

'Never.'

'Ever?' he checked, for she sounded so adamant.

'Never, ever.'

'Why not?'

She looked into the fire and wondered how to answer him. Naomi never told her employers her real reason for declining.

She would never even consider staying on. In fact, it was stipulated in the terms of her employment that a permanent nanny be signed to take over before Naomi commenced her role. And should that fall through, it was specified that an agency be used, for she would not be extending her contract.

No matter how wonderful the terms or the family.

Actually, because of just that.

'Why don't you stay in one place?' he asked again, and now he did probe, because suddenly Abe really wanted to know some more about her.

'I guess because I've never stayed in one place for very long. We do what we're used to, I suppose. Revert to type...'

But he shook his head at her excuses.

Abe wasn't buying it.

'Why?' he asked again.

He was brilliant at maths, but she didn't add up.

Abe wasn't one for sitting talking by a fire, but she'd made him feel at ease, she made the place feel like a home, yet she chose not to have one for herself.

'You want to know why?' She looked at him then, blue eyes on black as they held the other's gaze.

'Yes.'

'Because I'd fall in love with the family,' Naomi said. 'And then one day it would be time for me to leave.'

Her blue eyes were serious, and there was no trace of tears, which told him this was no revelation, she had known this about herself for a very long while.

Naomi twisted his heart in a way no one else could, and a hell of a lot had tried.

She twisted a heart that Abe hadn't even known he had.

He wanted to reach for her.

It was as instinctive as that.

And he wanted to chase her loneliness away in the only way he knew how.

Abe looked down at her full lips, all shiny from the food they had shared, and he wondered about her pepperoni kisses and just laying her down and taking her by the fire.

He wouldn't.

Not just because he had a conscience.

Abe had long thought his conscience had been severed along with the umbilical cord.

No, he wouldn't make a move because there was something so rare about tonight.

Something he didn't want to jeopardise.

And there was *nothing* he wanted her to regret.

Naomi felt the burn of his gaze and she felt the shift in the atmosphere.

The way he first held her eyes and then the lowering of them as they took in her mouth had her body prickling with sudden awareness.

Naomi had never encountered a moment such as this.

Just for a second, when rational thought was suspended, she wanted to know the feel of his mouth, and there was a sense of certainty that if he leant forward a fraction, then so too would she.

There was silence, save for the hiss and occasional spit from the fire and the tick of a clock on the mantel, yet she could hear the roar of blood in her ears and she almost closed her eyes in anticipation of bliss.

But Abe did not move forward. Instead, she watched as he looked away and reached for his drink, and so inexperienced was she that Naomi was certain she'd misread things.

Jet lag, cognac, and an absolute dearth of knowledge about men told Naomi that she'd been imagining things, and had come very close to looking a fool. She blushed as she pictured herself sitting, eyes closed, and waiting for a kiss that would never come. Embarrassed, she told herself that if she was having fantasies about a playboy wanting her, then it really was time for bed.

'I ought to get some sleep,' Naomi said. 'I've got a load of sightseeing planned for tomorrow.'

She stood and re-fastened the tie on her robe then reached for the box. 'Leave it,' he said, because if she bent down to retrieve it, he might just pull her in.

''Night, Abe.'

''Night.'

She made her way up the staircase and found her door, holding it together until in she was in the bedroom. But once there she sat on the bed and, head in hands, Naomi moaned.

Not because she'd foolishly thought he'd been about to kiss her. She could easily talk herself down from that—he was surely one of New York's most eligible bachelors, and there was no way he'd be interested in her.

No, it was because of how *she* felt.

In the space of an hour Naomi knew she had developed a king-sized crush on Abe and that was something she didn't want or need. Not just because she was here to work and nothing must get in the way of that, but because she was scared of being hurt.

Naomi guarded her heart with the same ferocity that she guarded her tiny charges.

There had been no dates, no romance in her life.

Her career took care of that, and she was grateful for it, especially on a night such as this.

She simply refused to open herself up to potential hurt.

CHAPTER THREE

ABE.

Naomi knew *exactly* where she was the very second that she awoke, and her first thought was about last night.

It was as if, in the hours since they had said goodnight, Abe Devereux had not left her mind.

Of course, she had surely left his.

She had overslept and it was after nine. No doubt he was at work now and not even thinking of their lazy fireside conversation on her very first night in New York.

Naomi was, though.

She'd heard of the Devereuxes before Merida had met Ethan. She had worked with a prominent family in London who'd had dealings with them. Now that she thought on it, Abe's name had been bandied about at the time. And not fondly. He was the gatekeeper to the Devereuxes. The one you had to get past if you wanted a deal to go through.

And when it came to women, his reputation had been equally formidable.

That was all she knew.

When she'd been trying to work out the dynamics of family, in order to best help her friend, Naomi had tended to skim past the articles on Abe.

Still, she recalled enough to know that that it wasn't just a case of lock up your daughters when Abe Devereux was around.

Lock up your wife too.

And possibly the nanny!

He had no scruples, that much she knew.

Determined not to dwell on him, Naomi reached for her phone and looked at the weather forecast.

Snow, with more snow to come.

It would have been so much easier to lie under the covers for a while longer but Naomi was very used to forcing herself out of bed and did so today. Her hair she left down and didn't worry about make-up. She rarely did. There wasn't much point when working with babies. She decided on black jeans and a huge silver-grey jumper as well as black boots, which she pulled on while sitting on her bed. Naomi topped it all off with her less-than-substantial jacket. Before heading out she would add a woolly hat along with her scarf, but for now she carried them down the stairs and headed into the kitchen.

And then nearly dropped them when she saw Abe

sitting on a breakfast stool, drinking coffee and reading on his tablet.

'Morning.' Barb smiled. 'How did you sleep?'

'Very well,' Naomi said. 'In fact, I overslept.'

'You're not the only one,' Barb said, and she glanced over at Abe, who didn't look up. 'You got a pizza in the night, I see. You could have called me for something to eat if you were hungry. Come and sit down and have some breakfast…' And then she must have remembered that Naomi was actually a guest. 'Or take a seat in the dining room and—'

'I don't eat breakfast,' Naomi said quickly.

That was a complete lie.

Naomi loved breakfast and the first café she saw she was finding a bagel, but she was a touch flustered by Abe's presence and trying not to show it. She hadn't expected to see him, and certainly, if he'd still been here, she hadn't expected him to be sitting in the kitchen. 'I'm actually heading out.'

She kept reminding herself there was nothing to be flustered about.

Except, far from relaxed, as she had been last night, the sight and scent of him, freshly showered, with damp hair and all clean shaven, was doing the oddest thing to her heart rate. She felt like a teenager.

An awkward one at that.

And Barb would not let her go.

'You're not leaving this house without a coffee

at least,' Barb said, as she poured her one from the pot. 'Cream?'

'Just black, please.'

As Barb poured she chatted to Abe and it became clear he'd been updating her on Jobe. 'Is there anything I can make for him?'

'I don't think so,' he said, only glancing up from his tablet. 'I'll let you know, but really he's not eating much.'

'Ginger's good for nausea,' Barb said, and then turned her attention to Naomi. 'So, what are your plans for today? I sure hope you're not going out in just that jacket.'

'I'm buying a coat,' Naomi *again* explained. 'I'm heading to a department store first.'

'I'll call Bernard to drive you.'

'There's no need.' Naomi shook her head. 'I really want to walk. The baby may well be home tomorrow or the day after that so I want to see as much as I can today. I can give you a hand tonight with the tree, though…'

'A hand?' Barb checked. 'I shan't be decorating it…' She laughed at the very thought. 'We'll leave that to the experts. You just enjoy your day and don't worry about us.'

Abe carried on reading as Barb and Naomi chatted and it would seem she had rather high expectations of all she could cram in today.

Especially on foot.

'I want to see the tree at the Rockefeller Center, and I want to see the window displays…' She reeled things off as Abe sat there, reading. 'I really wanted to see feed the squirrels in Central Park but they'll be hibernating—oh, and I want to walk over Brooklyn Bridge.'

'Today?' Barb checked.

'Well, not *all* of it today,' Naomi said. 'I'll have to get a map and plot it out. I'm useless at following directions on my phone.'

'I've got one somewhere.'

As Barb bustled off to find it she was left with Abe, and Naomi had to remind herself there was nothing to feel awkward about.

She just did.

The air felt a little warmer, so much so that as she pulled on her hat she decided the scarf could wait until she was at the front door.

And then, without looking up, Abe spoke.

'Squirrels don't hibernate.'

It took a moment to register he was commenting on her conversation with Barb.

'I think you'll find that they do,' Naomi said, and now he looked up, those gorgeous black eyes meeting hers.

'And I'm certain you'll find that they don't.'

There was a small stand-off.

Abe watched her lips open to argue, but he was

more than sure he was right. 'You can apologise to me tonight once you've found out I'm right.'

Two things in that statement surprised Abe.

That he could be bothered to debate the hibernation habits of squirrels.

And that he was already thinking about tonight.

Especially when she gave up arguing and a smile spread over her lips.

'So I *can* feed them?' Naomi checked, nerves forgotten now, for he made conversation so easy and despite his officious tone he simply made her smile.

'Yes.'

'What should I get?'

'Get?'

'For them to eat?'

'You can buy nuts there.'

'Oh.'

'Hot ones. Fit for human consumption.'

'Yum,' Naomi said. 'But first I need to head to Macy's for my coat.'

'There are stores other than Macy's.'

'No, it has to be that one.'

'Why?'

'So that when I'm asked where I got my gorgeous coat, I won't sound pretentious by saying New York. I'll just say Macy's, but they'll know.'

'I see.' He didn't. 'If you can wait five minutes, I'm leaving. I can have my driver drop you there.'

'But I want to walk.'

She had no idea the size of the place, Abe thought. 'Walk once you have a coat.'

Naomi knew she should say no to his offer, just as she had with Barb.

And that she should keep as much distance as possible between them and remind herself to shield her heart, because this crush on Abe was blowing up in her chest like a bouncy castle inflating. And, yes, away from him she was wary, but when they spoke, when he looked right at her all the warnings tumbled away and she just fell into conversation with him, forgot that she was usually awkward around men, and she forgot too to feel big and clumsy.

The rules Naomi generally lived by did not seem to apply when she was *with* Abe.

'Okay,' she conceded with a smile. 'While you're there, you could get something for Ava.'

'I've already given the baby a present and…' He halted. Abe had been about to point out that his driver would be taking her to Macy's *after* he'd been dropped off at work, but now that he thought about it a couple of hours off sounded appealing. Khalid was expecting him to call and, Abe decided, a well-timed unexplained absence might be in order to remind the Sheikh who was boss!

He drained his coffee. 'Come on, then.'

As they were driven, it was nice to take a familiar route with someone who was so excited by *every-*

thing. Even tiny things like overhead traffic lights got a mention. 'It looks just like I'd imagined it but better,' Naomi said.

'It looks just like it always does,' Abe said, but he did pull his eyes away from his tablet and stopped scrolling through the mountain of emails that had accumulated overnight and stared out at the city he loved.

The horses and carriages were all lined up, and the streets were bustling.

'I fell asleep on the way from the airport,' Naomi explained, 'so I didn't see anything yesterday.'

And now he regretted not going yesterday to meet her and sending a car instead.

Abe didn't do regret, yet for a second there he did. Not that she let him linger in it—Naomi had far too many questions.

'Have you done your Christmas shopping?' she asked.

'I don't do all that.'

'What, you do it online?'

'No, I don't do it online. I just don't do Christmas. Well, there's the Christmas Eve ball and I give Jessica, my PA, a weekend away, but that's about it.'

She was appalled. 'What about your father? Surely you get him a present?'

'What could he possibly need?' Abe asked, but as she opened her mouth he got there first. 'I'll think of something.'

'Good.'

'What do you want for Christmas?' Naomi asked.

'Peace and quiet,' Abe said, and, to her credit, she laughed. 'We're here.'

So they were.

'You couldn't have walked it,' he pointed out as they pulled up at the iconic store.

'I could have,' Naomi insisted as she got out of the car. 'I'll walk back instead.' She stood and looked up at the magnificent building, dressed for Christmas with red and green bows. People were already crowded at the windows, looking at the displays. 'Oh, my goodness. I can't believe I'm really here.'

'Your coat awaits.'

Abe had on his own coat.

It was a long black woollen one worn over his suit, but once they had agreed where to meet and Naomi had wandered off, Abe saw that he was being noticed and decided that a wool hat of his own might be in order. He didn't want to be constantly recognised all day, or for his sightseeing trip to be captured on someone's phone just to be sold to the papers and all the palaver that would cause.

And, yes, he was taking the day off, and called Jessica as he took the escalator.

'What should I say to Khalid?' Jessica responded, clearly perplexed, because there was not a single Devereux in the office today, and that hadn't happened in all the time she'd been there.

'That I'm unavailable,' Abe clipped.

'Felicia and her entourage are here for you,' Jessica said. 'To measure you for next season as well as the Devereux Ball.'

Abe wasn't listening. For the first time in what felt like for ever his mind wasn't on work. In fact, his eyes were drawn to the most ridiculous, huge, pink bear with big black eyes, as black as Ava's would undoubtedly be someday.

'Sort it,' Abe said, and rang off.

He thought of what Naomi had said, about the type of uncle he wanted to be. It had never entered his mind he might be the uncle-bearing-teddy-bears type. But if you couldn't buy a giant pink bear for your one-day-old niece, who could you buy one for?

And that was how she next saw him.

Naomi was wearing the most gorgeous new red coat and held a large bag containing things pink. Pink sleepsuits, a pink blanket and also a little sleepsuit in a bright cherry red, the same shade as her coat. She was standing happily watching the world go by as she mentally planned the rest of her day, but then she saw Abe, standing on the escalator, wearing a black hat and holding a huge pink bear. He wasn't smiling. Instead, he looked moody and scowling, and on seeing him her first thought was, *Help!*

Help! Naomi thought again, as he caught sight of her and smiled and walked over.

Please get on with being the utter bastard I've been warned that you are.

But help wasn't arriving.

'Nice coat,' he said, which in itself wasn't a problem.

More it was the approval in his eyes and the flurry it set off in her chest.

They loaded the bear into his car but, instead of saying goodbye to her, the driver was sent on his way, and it took a moment for Naomi to register that Abe was going to be her tour guide for the day.

'To make up for not picking you up at the airport,' he offered by way of explanation.

'Really?'

'Ethan asked me to, but I had a lot of meetings yesterday.'

'And you don't today?'

'Nope,' he said. 'Well, I should go in, but there are a few issues and it might serve me better…' He hesitated, because certainly he shared business matters with no one. 'I forgot you were friends with Merida for a moment there.'

'Oh, not you too,' Naomi huffed. 'I've got Barb backing off because I'm not real "staff" and now you…'

'Really?' he said, genuinely intrigued. 'What would Barb tell you if you weren't a friend of Merida's?'

'The gossip.' Naomi smiled.

And on a slushy, wet street they faced each other.

'Well, I don't have gossip as such,' Abe said. 'Just a headache developing in the Middle East. One that I don't want my brother to know about just yet.'

'My lips are sealed.'

He wished they weren't.

As he looked down at them, Abe rather wished he was prising them open with his tongue, and possibly she was thinking the same thing because she pressed them together in response to the sudden scrutiny.

'So,' Abe said, rather than do something very un-Abe-like and kiss her in the middle of the street, 'I've got a clear day, so if you want company…'

'I'd love it.'

And he was wonderful, wonderful company.

Naomi did her share of sightseeing on her days off, wherever she went, but always alone.

On this cold, cold day, she was embraced by his company as they first took in the breath-taking Christmas window displays filled with enchanting scenes.

Abe didn't hover at the back or subtly nudge in, he moved straight to the front and took her with him. Every window told a story. There were fairies waving their wands and trains made of candy and the sounds of delighted children's laughter and music playing brought tears to her eyes.

For the first time it was starting to feel like Christmas should, Naomi thought.

She could gaze at the displays for ever but it

seemed they had a schedule to adhere to! 'Ready?' Abe said.

'For what?'

The Empire State Building was what!

And, because it was December, they didn't have to line up and soon they were on the top of the world, or rather, Naomi corrected herself, the top of New York City. 'But it feels like the top of the world.'

'Actually, my office is higher.'

'I don't believe you.' Naomi smiled, stamping her feet against the cold and digging her hands into the pockets of her coat. She had never felt so cold, or so exhilarated and happy, all at the same time.

He pointed out landmarks and the bridges and the snow had thinned enough that she could see the Statue of Liberty.

'I'm going to do one of the river cruises on my day off,' Naomi said.

'You'll freeze.'

'I don't care.' Naomi laughed.

From up high she did her best to get her bearings in a snow-blanketed city. 'So, you live that way?' She pointed.

'No,' Abe corrected, 'my father lives there and…' he guided her by the elbow to the other side '…I live there at Greenwich Village. See the green?' She followed to where he pointed. 'That's Washington Square Park and the view from my bedroom window.'

'Oh, I'd love to see it…' Naomi said, but it came

out wrong. 'I meant Greenwich Village is on my to-do list…' *Not* the view from his bedroom window.

'I know what you meant.'

He gave her a smile and it felt as if the snow stopped and even the wind eased as he corrected her little faux pas. Except it didn't feel like one, it felt more like a Freudian slip.

From the giddy heights of the Empire State Building they moved on to the Rockefeller Center and the gigantic tree, and, yes, he took her photo in front of it. As he finished, a German tourist asked if they'd like one together, and would he mind taking theirs, *bitte*?

It was easier to just say yes, or *ja*, than to explain to a stranger that they weren't, in fact, a couple.

And as they stood side by side, and the German tourist waved them to move closer and he put an arm around her, Naomi found her smile a touch stilted for the very first time that day.

It was all just so amazing, so wonderful that Naomi knew, just knew, she'd be looking at this photo for a very long time to come.

CHAPTER FOUR

It was her perfect day.

In every way.

There was so much to see and do and they crammed in all they could.

'I should have bought some gloves,' Naomi said, blowing into her hands as they wandered down Madison Avenue, but Abe had a trick for that and bought them huge pretzels, hot from the cart, and they warmed their hands very nicely.

'My dad taught me that,' Abe said. 'Though I think it was more that he loved to eat them.'

'You did some nice things with your dad.'

'We did,' he admitted, and stole a look at her and wondered why this amazing woman had no one. And how come she had no family?

And so he pried, only it didn't feel that way to him. He just had to know.

'Do you, did you…?' He watched as she braced herself, no doubt used to the question, so he rephrased it. 'Do you have any memories at all of your family?'

'Not good ones,' Naomi said, and she peeled off some warm dough but didn't put it in her mouth. Instead, she told him the truth. 'I've never seen my mother. I tried contacting her when I was old enough to, but she didn't want to know.'

'Then she missed out,' Abe said, but it sounded like a trite response and he knew it so he tried again. 'Maybe it was for the best.'

'I doubt it.'

'Some people shouldn't be parents,' Abe said, and he shared with her something he had never, ever shared with anyone. Not with his father, not with Ethan. Oh, they knew it, of course, but he'd never said it out loud. 'My mother was one of them.'

Naomi knew that she was hearing the truth, rather than being placated. And she knew, too, that he was sharing a very private part of his rather public life.

'And,' Abe added, only this time, given what he'd just shared, it didn't sound trite, 'she *did* miss out—I can't imagine anything nicer than a day spent with you.'

It was possibly the nicest thing he could have said to her.

They stood on a busy street but it might just as well have been empty because it felt as if it was just the two of them. Then, not used to too much disclosure, he peeled off some dough and popped it into his mouth. 'Come on,' he said. 'Lots to see...'

He fought not to take her hand and Naomi had to ball hers into a fist so as not to reach for his.

And so, rather than make herself look a fool, she peered into a very well-dressed window. 'Now, *that's* a coat!'

It was long and the deepest shade of violet, perhaps more of a velvet cape than a coat.

It was absolutely exquisite.

'I'm supposed to be get measured up,' Abe said, thinking of the fitter he had blown off today and deciding that while they were here to just get it over and done with. 'Let's go in.'

Naomi would never, in a million years, have entered such a place and neither would she have been greeted as warmly. But as she was with Abe the blonde and groomed sales associate was very amenable.

'Mr Devereux!'

'Felicia.' Abe's return greeting was less effusive, but it didn't matter. Of course, he was told, it wasn't a problem that he'd missed the private appointment that had been scheduled to take place in his office earlier today.

'I was just speaking with Jessica,' Felicia said with a smile, 'and trying to arrange another time. Let's get you measured. Will your, er...' She glanced at Naomi and clearly didn't know how to place her, but she gave it a go. 'Will your assistant be coming through?'

It was the only awkward moment.

Well, it was for Naomi.

Of course, they would never think she might simply be *with* him and merely assumed that she was one of his staff.

'I'll just look around,' Naomi said, declining the offer of refreshments and looking at the stunning outfits that were completely beyond her reach, though it was heaven to gaze. Still, she did wonder how long it took to be measured when, half an hour later, she was still looking around.

'It shouldn't be too much longer,' Felicia said.

As it turned out, Mr Devereux wasn't just selecting a tux for the ball. There were swatches and buttons and collars and cuffs for suits that would see him to summer.

'How long have you worked for the Devereuxes?' Felicia asked as they chatted.

'Oh, I don't work for them,' Naomi corrected her. 'We're just…' she didn't really know what to say, so possibly she took a slight leap in her description '…friends.'

Well, they were acquaintances perhaps.

Two people who had one person, Merida, who connected them. Still, she wasn't about to explain all that to Felicia.

But in that moment *everything* changed.

The slightly casual air to their conversation disappeared and suddenly, now she was no longer mere staff, Felicia was on higher alert. 'You like the wrap?' she asked, when Naomi's hands lingered on a length of fabric so soft it felt like mercury running through her hand.

'I love it,' Naomi said.

'There's a dress,' Felicia said. 'It would go with your colouring.'

'Oh, I doubt that it comes in my size.'

Felicia was actually very skilled at her job. So much so that twenty minutes later Naomi stood in high heels with the gorgeous floor-length dress on, and, lo, it did come in her size.

'You look,' Felicia said, 'stunning.'

'Ah, but you're paid to say that.'

'No.' Felicia shook her head. 'I don't want anyone wearing something from our range if they don't suit it and absolutely you do.'

Did she?

It was nice to dream. It was just dress-up and fun, and, no, not for Abe's eyes, but she came out of the dressing room smiling.

In contrast, Abe was scowling.

'I didn't think it would take that long.' He rolled his eyes as they headed out. 'Just how many shades of black are there?'

Naomi laughed.

Her happiness remained, even heightened as the

sun sank lower and Naomi found out that, yes, there were still squirrels in winter in Central Park.

At first there was just one that she could see as Abe headed off and bought some nuts.

'They're for the squirrels,' Abe reminded her, when Naomi had a taste.

'There aren't any.'

Except then she saw one, sitting upright in the snow.

She tossed him a nut and very boldly he came and took it and then scuttled off.

'There's one,' Abe said, and he took some nuts and threw them, and then there was another.

And another.

They came very close, right up onto the benches, and Naomi laughed as she fed them nuts and some even took them from her fingers.

Abe took some photos on her phone.

'This is like a dream come true.' Naomi was beside herself. There were squirrels coming from everywhere.

She looked like Snow White, Abe thought, but of course didn't say so. 'Was I right?' Abe checked. 'Or was I right?'

'You were right, Abe,' Naomi teased. 'Squirrels don't hibernate and I apologise for ever doubting you.' And she took them back to their conversation and neither could believe it had been just this morning, because after a day spent together it felt like a long time ago.

'You missed that one,' Abe said, pointing out a little black little squirrel who held back from the others.

'He won't come…' Naomi said, because she'd already noticed the little creature, who shook and startled but clearly wanted to join in. Finally, with coaxing, he came over and had his share of the little packet of nuts.

'Do you want to get some more?' Abe offered.

'Another time,' Naomi said. 'I can't feel my feet.'

It was growing dark and it was utterly freezing so some real food and serious warming up was called for. 'Do you want to go for a drink?' he offered as he handed her back her phone and they walked towards the park's exit. 'Or perhaps an early dinner? We could go over to the Plaza?'

He nodded in the direction of the gorgeous building and it was an invitation she could scarcely comprehend.

'I'm hardly dressed for the Plaza,' Naomi pointed out. Her coat might be gorgeous but beneath that she wore jeans and the bottoms of them were drenched.

'It doesn't matter.'

And it wouldn't matter, Naomi knew.

She could be dressed in sackcloth and ashes and they would make the exception for him. But it mattered to Naomi—she knew she must look a fright. It was better to leave things here, Naomi decided, to simply end their perfect day. And she had the perfect excuse too… 'I promised Merida I'd be in to visit this evening.'

Perhaps it was for the best, Abe thought.

He too was supposed to be at the hospital.

In the space of a day he'd gone from wearing a hat so he wasn't recognised to offering to step out together in the Plaza.

It could only cause trouble.

On *so* many levels.

'I'm going to go back to the house and get changed,' Naomi said, 'and then head to the hospital.'

'Well, I'll call my driver.' Abe took out his phone and did just that. 'I'll head to the hospital now and drop you home on the way.'

'Sounds good,' Naomi agreed. 'Abe, thank you for the most wonderful day. I wouldn't have seen half as much if you hadn't been with me.' Though it was more than the sights she had seen that had made it so special. 'It's been amazing,' she said.

'It has,' he agreed.

'How's your Middle East headache now?' she asked.

'Gone!' he said. 'Though probably not for long. I bet Ethan's found out.'

'Found out what?'

He smiled at her persistence. 'Khalid and Ethan are friends. They went to college together. I warned Ethan not to mix business and friendship.'

'It can work.'

'Not in my book.' He shook his head. 'Khalid has helped pave our way into expanding into the Middle East, I admit that, but it's a business agreement and one he'll benefit from enormously. I refuse to be beholden to him. He's got feet in both camps.'

'I don't understand.'

'Well, he's a partner in our Middle Eastern branch, but he's also Prince of the country where we're looking to extend.'

'So he's got both your interests at heart.'

He gave a wry laugh. 'It makes better business sense to view him as screwing us out of millions than looking out for his people.'

'Perhaps,' Naomi said. 'It's nicer to think of it the other way around, though.'

'I don't play nice.'

'You did today,' Naomi said.

'Today was an exception.'

Or rather today had for Abe been exceptional.

He felt as if he'd been born fighting. Keeping one eye out for Ethan and another on his mother. And later there had been no halcyon days to his youth. Just the weight of the Devereux name and the depraved reputation he upheld.

Today, in the midst of the darkest times, it had felt as if the world as he knew it had been put on hold.

He stopped walking, they both did, and turned

and faced each other. Naomi looked down as he took her hands in his.

Finally.

Oh, they'd been blown on and thrust deep into pockets, and wrapped around hot pretzels and bags of nuts, and all day they had resisted this. So many times he had wanted to reach for hers, and all day her hands had felt as if they had secretly sought his.

Now they met and she watched his fingers wrap around hers and felt the warmth that came not just from his skin but from the surge in her heart.

She was here in New York to work, and usually Naomi did not do foolish things such as get involved with family, and she always guarded her heart, but all that faded when she met his eyes.

There was gentle snow and there *were* squirrels and there was a hush that descended over a noisy city as his mouth neared hers. His scent was close, not quite familiar yet, and she imprinted on her mind the heady notes as she breathed him in.

The first intimate touch sent a slight tremor through Naomi, but then came a flutter of relief as their mouths met, for it felt as if she had waited for ever to know this bliss.

She had.

Abe Devereux's was her very first kiss, and the first time she had lowered the gates to her heart.

He sensed it.

Abe felt her slight jolt at the first contact, and then

her untutored return to the caress of his mouth. And he fathomed only then that this kiss was her first. The magnitude of that had him hold back a fraction, his approach now more tender, lest he startle her again.

Kissing was usually a means to an end to Abe.

A mere precursor to bed.

He did not hold hands in public, let alone kiss in a park, yet there was no thought to his surroundings at that moment. Just that her lips were cold so he must warm them. He felt her hesitancy mingled with shivering want, and she reminded him of that little squirrel, nervous and cautious yet yearning.

Abe made her yearn.

The pressure of his lips was sublime. He dropped her hands and wrapped his arms around her, and winter disappeared as he pulled her closer into his strength and warmth and she was cradled in the arms of bliss. Her lips parted without thought, lost to his kiss, but then came the next shock, the feel of his tongue, which had her head pulling back, but his hand was exerting slight pressure there, and after a second she sank into the stupor of his deepening kiss and the feather-light strokes that stirred her inside.

Naomi gave in to the sweet and sensual pleasure of mouths mingling, tasting and exploring each other, and she savoured each sensation, from the surprising softness of his mouth to the slight scratch of his lightly stubbled jaw, which increased as he kissed her harder, their mouths more insistent, and she knew what to do now.

As pleasure and want merged, she moaned and he swallowed it, guiding her generous hips into his with the palm of his hand, and then held her in a sensual embrace.

She felt a new hunger, one she had never known before, unfurl inside her. And when he had kissed her so hard that she was breathless, when he had taken her from hesitant to urgent with the stroke of his tongue, he pulled back.

Abe had no choice but to do that for the feel of her in his arms dictated a need for more, and the strength of their kiss had to be severed, for decency's sake.

Their foreheads rested against each other's, and he could feel her breasts against his chest as her breathing refused to calm, and the shock of how good a kiss could be was Abe's now.

'I've been wanting to do that since last night,' Abe said, their lips still almost touching, and she let out a small laugh.

'I've been hoping you would,' Naomi admitted, relieved that she hadn't been imagining things after all. That this knowing, sensual man had been feeling the same way she had.

His arms held her steady and Naomi looked up at him and, quite simply, if he took her hand now, and if somehow there could be a magical bed, then he could lead her to it.

For Naomi, it was a revelation.

Till now she had never been kissed, never been close enough to another to touch them intimately, let alone consider sharing a man's bed.

And when he released her, when the world rushed in, so too did doubt.

He could hurt her, her mind warned.

Hush, her heart said.

He pulled out his phone and read a text informing him the car was here. 'We'll speak tonight,' Abe told her.

They sat apart in the car, and not just because of the giant teddy commanding its own seat, but because it was just all too new and too complicated to fathom, let alone share with the world.

But she was floating, and wondering how to deal with Merida and Ethan and, gosh, how to tell this suave man that she'd never slept with anyone before.

Yes, she was certain that this was where it was leading.

'Thank you,' Naomi said, as she got out of the car.

It felt a little paltry to offer such bland thanks for giving her the very best day but she kept things polite and smiled at Barb as she was let into the house.

'How was your day, exploring?' Barb asked.

'Marvellous.'

'Was that Abe's driver that dropped you off?'

'Yes,' Naomi answered as casually as she could.

'He said to let him know when I was finished sightseeing, and that he'd give me a ride back…' Then she stopped having to think up excuses as she was suddenly blindsided by the tree. 'Oh, my…'

It was pink.

Yet it was still elegant.

There were pale pink snowflakes that looked like blossoms dotted on the branches, and pale pink baubles that were so delicate that they looked like they might pop like bubbles if she so much as breathed.

'It's heavenly,' Naomi said, but there really wasn't time to dwell too long. 'I really have to get changed and then head to the hospital. I'll get a cab…'

'No need, Bernard will take you.'

Before she changed, Naomi sat on the bed for a moment and tried to steady herself, because when she was away from him she felt fat and uncertain and it all felt impossible.

You're here to work, she told herself.

But she had a life too.

One that had been devoid of men.

Devoid of passion.

Devoid of love.

And it was too soon to be even thinking that, but every part of this was new to Naomi.

So instead of panicking about the impossibility of it all she pulled on dry jeans and a black jumper, and as she did so she recalled his kiss.

And while she tried to reel herself in, her heart felt

as if it was rolling out and she ran down the stairs on a cloud of excitement about all the night might hold.

Bernard, as it turned out, was Barb's husband and had been Jobe's driver. 'I've driven him for close to twenty-five years,' he told Naomi as he drove her to the hospital. 'Barb started working for him after Mrs Devereux passed and then he took me on as his driver. We were going to stay for two years,' he told her as he pulled up at the hospital. 'That was the plan.'

Naomi was about to laugh and say something about the best-laid plans, but it died on her lips when she saw his strained face and remembered that tonight not everyone felt as happy as she did. He must be so terribly sad about Jobe, and perhaps worried about his and Barb's future.

'It's such a difficult time,' Naomi said, and Bernard nodded.

'It's great news about the baby, though.'

'It is,' Naomi agreed.

'I'll wait for you here.'

'Thank you.'

Naomi headed into the private wing and, having shown her ID, was let through to see Merida, who was rather more flustered than yesterday.

'How are you?' Naomi asked.

'Fine, but she's not feeding and they said she needs to go under the lights. That she's got jaundice.'

It was all completely normal, but for Merida completely overwhelming, and Naomi took her time to reassure her that all was well, but Merida was worried about Naomi too. 'I feel terrible that you're here and rattling around the house on your own.'

'Don't be daft,' Naomi said. 'Barb and Bernard have been lovely and I've been out sightseeing today.' She had already decided not to mention that her day had been spent with Abe.

In fact, she would have to work out when, or even if, she would tell Merida.

For now, though, she focussed on the baby, who was crying and hungry. 'Try and relax,' Naomi said as she positioned her to feed. 'Maybe try talking to me while you feed her.'

And it worked, because as Merida chatted about all that had been going on between her and Ethan, she relaxed and so too did little Ava.

'I know you've been so worried about our marriage, and in truth so have I, but things are going really well. I know you must be thinking it's just in the rush of Ava being born, but it was before that. We talked, I mean, we really talked. I think this is a new start for us.'

'I'm so happy for you.'

'We *both* want this marriage to work.'

She looked down at her baby. 'I'm so glad that Jobe got to see her. Ethan and he are finally talking…'

'But they work together,' Naomi pointed out.

'I mean, they're finally close. There's some stuff

with the mother that I found out…' She didn't elaborate and Naomi didn't push—in fact, her eyes came to rest on the huge teddy bear.

'Abe brought that in for Ava this evening,' Merida said when she saw where Naomi was looking. 'Hard to believe. There must be a heart in there somewhere…'

'Everybody's nice if you give them a chance.'

Merida shook her head 'Not Abe. He's an island. And a hostile, uninhabitable one at that.'

And Naomi had no choice but to listen as Merida spoke on.

'Honestly, the way he works his way through women… I don't know how Candice puts up with him.'

'Candice?' Naomi checked. She'd heard that name, or rather she was sure that she had read it somewhere as she'd skimmed articles on Abe during her research into the Devereux family. She had only really been trying to find out about Ethan, so she could help her friend.

So, who was Candice?

Merida soon answered. 'Abe's partner.'

Thankfully Merida was looking down at Ava so she didn't see the look of horror wash over Naomi's face.

'His partner?' Naomi echoed, struggling to keep her voice even.

'Yes, they've been together for a couple of years.'

'They're *still* together?'

Merida frowned at either the sudden inflection or the sudden interest in Abe Devereux's love life and Naomi had to think quickly. 'It's just I thought I'd read somewhere that they'd broken up.'

'You probably did.' Merida nodded. 'They're always breaking up—he constantly cheats and she always ends up taking him back, but, no, they're definitely together. She came in to visit with him tonight.' Merida looked up. 'Believe me when I say he's an utter bastard.'

Oh, Naomi believed her.

She had just found that out for herself.

CHAPTER FIVE

ABE HAD A PARTNER!

Merida's words had left Naomi reeling but she'd had to remain calm and dig deep to smile her way through the rest of the visit.

That didn't end at visiting time, though, when she wished she could walk home from the hospital, if only to gather her thoughts. Instead, after a visit spent reassuring Merida, and with her own head spinning, Naomi stepped out of the hospital to the car waiting for her.

She wanted to cry but she refused to.

More than that she wanted to erase the day. Her wonderful, beautiful day, she simply wanted it gone, and to never, ever have known how it felt to be held and kissed by Abe, and to be utterly fooled by those dark eyes.

So she chatted away to Bernard on the drive back and then the door opened and there was Barb, anxious for news about mother and baby.

'How's Merida?' she asked as Naomi took off her coat.

'She's doing well.'

'And little Ava?' Barb checked, taking the coat and clearly anxious for a more detailed update.

'Gorgeous.'

'Will they be home tomorrow?'

Her mind felt as if it was wading through mud just to formulate a response. 'I think it might be a couple more days,' Naomi said, and then she saw Abe, coming out of the drawing room. His jacket and tie were off and he was holding a glass. He looked exquisite. She quickly jerked her eyes away, refusing to even allow herself that thought.

'I've got dinner ready for you…' Barb said, and her voice seemed to be coming from a long way away. She could feel Abe's eyes on her.

'That's lovely, but I'm really tired. I've walked for miles today and I think jet lag has finally caught up with me.'

She knew.

Instantly, Abe was certain that she had found out about Candice. He could tell from her pinched expression and the way she turned away from him.

Damn!

Candice had met him at the hospital, as had previously been arranged, except he'd forgotten. His driver had dropped him off, and there, beside the elevators to the private wing, had been Candice.

'What the hell is that?' she had asked when she'd seen the bear.

'It's for my niece.'

'Well, it would hardly be for me.'

As arranged, they had gone in to visit together.

He had spent years fashioning his life, and only Candice, himself and Abe's private attorney knew of the deal they had agreed to.

He had admitted to Ethan the truth of their status, but that had been on the night he had told him that Merida was pregnant and Abe had attempted to show his brother that there were other ways to deal with the situation than marriage, but they had never discussed it since.

Abe's seeming relationship with Candice was a business arrangement. Her stability and presence appeased the board, but they hadn't slept together in years.

Their arrangement allowed a veneer of respectability to put a layer of gloss over his rather debauched life.

He housed her in an Upper East Side apartment and paid her a generous monthly allowance and, in return, she seemingly stood by his side.

Certainly, it was not something he shared with someone he'd had one kiss with.

It was not something he'd ever intended to share with anyone.

He waited till Barb had taken her coat and had headed off before he attempted to speak to her.

'Naomi…'

She ignored him and headed up the stairs.

Possibly not the most adult way of dealing with things but, hell, Naomi just wanted to process what she'd found out alone, and work out how she felt about it all, before having to deal with him.

'Naomi!' He called her name more sharply and came to the bottom of the stairs, and she had the feeling he wouldn't hesitate to follow her up.

'Yes?' She turned and attempted to look composed, but she looked past Abe's shoulder at the gorgeous tree rather than at him.

'Come through to the drawing room,' he said. 'It's more private in there.'

'We have nothing *private* to discuss,' Naomi answered. She didn't want to hear his excuses and lies, but more than that she wanted to be alone with her own thoughts and to assemble them into some sort of order before she discussed this with him.

But Abe was persistent. 'We need to talk.'

'I think we already did quite enough of that,' Naomi said. 'In fact, we spoke most of last night and all of today, and during all that time you refrained from telling me the one thing I should have known.'

'Can we not do this on the stairs?' Abe suggested.

'Can we simply not do this?' Naomi implored.

She loathed any sort of confrontation and, though she would never, ever admit it, despite her devastation, Naomi was just the tiniest bit relieved.

Yes, relieved that the feeling he evoked, the hope that had been gathering, could now safely lead… nowhere.

That she could reel in her heart right now, before it was too late.

She had learnt, long ago, how it felt to be discarded, to put down tentative roots and then be plucked up and moved along. Not so much in romance, she had no experience there. But in love, in family, at school and with friends, and she never wanted to revisit those feelings again.

And with that thought she was able to look him in the eye and dismiss the magical time they had shared. 'It was a day out. It was a kiss. Probably small change to you and I was tired from flying and…' She shrugged. 'Abe, I'm here to work and to be a friend to Merida. Can we please just forget it happened?'

'Naomi…'

But she had already walked off.

To Abe's discredit, he was just a touch relieved by her dismissal.

It had been a day out that had ended with a kiss, nothing more.

Certainly, it was nothing worth rocking the boat over.

God knew, there was enough else going on.

* * *

Abe was absent from the kitchen the next morning and again that night.

And he was absent in the two weeks that followed.

His name came up in various conversations, some Naomi was a part of, though most she was not.

'Abe's staying over at the hospital tonight,' she'd heard Ethan tell Barb on the day Ava had come home.

And when Ava was two weeks old, and Naomi and Merida were about to head over to the park, Ethan rang to say that Khalid was flying to NYC to sort out, face to face, the land sale issue.

'Don't ask,' Merida said, and rolled her eyes.

Naomi definitely didn't.

She was doing her level best to put the elder Devereux brother out of her mind.

And there was more than enough to be getting on with.

Merida was still struggling to feed Ava herself, and the baby was hungry and difficult to settle and liked to sleep the morning away and stay up all night.

Mid-afternoon, rather than have Merida give in and feed her again, they bundled her up in blankets and a hat and she lay screaming in her new pram.

'Isn't it too cold?' Merida checked.

'She's as warm as toast,' Naomi said. 'And they like the motion of the pram.'

Ava did.

She didn't sleep, but she did hush as they walked

the paths. The snow had let up and it was a crisp, sunny day as Merida told her just how difficult Naomi had been theh previous night.

'I don't want to take her into bed with me, but she takes the tiniest feed and then falls asleep. The second I put her down, she starts to cry.'

'Why don't you let me have her for the night?' Naomi suggested. 'I could bring her in four-hourly for feeds.'

'I want her with me.'

Abe, damn him, was right.

Business and friendships were best kept apart.

Oh, Naomi didn't consider her work as business as such, but she was professional in her role.

Usually her employers wanted a nanny.

Merida didn't.

She wanted her baby with her at night and though she was completely lovely, the fact was most new mothers didn't want their close friend around twenty-four seven as they stumbled through the first weeks of parenthood.

Had she not been paid to be there, Naomi might have suggested that she check into a hotel, or even just come for a week or two.

Not two months!

They came to the lake and sat down on the bench but almost as soon as they had, the lack of motion set Ava off.

'Let's walk,' Naomi suggested when she saw that Merida was close to tears.

'No, let's head back.'

Poor Merida was so exhausted that she took Naomi's suggestion that, rather than feed her, she head off for a sleep. 'I'll wake you at six,' Naomi said.

'I can't leave her crying till then.'

'She won't be,' Naomi said, rather hoping that was true.

Ava did her level best.

'Is she hungry?' Barb asked a couple of hours later when Naomi came into the kitchen with a screaming Ava over her shoulder.

'She wants to use her mum as a dummy,' Naomi said, then corrected herself so that Barb would understand. 'A pacifier. I'm hoping that if Merida can have a proper sleep and I can calm Ava down, they might get a good feed. I'll give her a bath soon and hopefully that will calm her.'

'Doesn't her crying bother you?' Barb asked.

'A bit,' Naomi admitted, 'but nowhere near as much it upsets Merida—she has the keys straight to her mother's heartstrings.'

But held upright and lulled by the conversation, Ava started to calm. 'What are you making?' Naomi asked Barb.

'Chicken soup, the proper way. For Jobe.'

Naomi smiled and decided to watch and see how

chicken soup was made the *proper* way. There was a whole chicken simmering in the pot, along with vegetables and herbs, and the kitchen smelt divine—it must have because, though awake, little Ava had stopped crying and was resting on Naomi's shoulder.

'Bernard will take it in later,' Barb said. 'And some for Abe too.'

'He's there a lot, is he?' Naomi couldn't help but check.

'He goes in after work and I think he's staying till late at night. I wish that he'd stop here afterwards, but he seems to have stopped doing that.'

Naomi swallowed. She really hoped that what had happened between Abe and her wasn't affecting his decisions. She doubted it, though. Of course she had looked him up online more thoroughly and it would seem a kiss in a park was extremely chaste compared to his other well-reported shenanigans over the years.

She doubted he had given it a second thought.

Whereas she thought about him all the time.

All the time.

Yet how could she not?

There were photos lining the walls and his name was dropped into the conversation numerous times. And each night she'd lain there, with ears on elastic, wondering if he might have decided to stay after he had visited the hospital.

It would seem that he hadn't.

'You came just after Mrs Devereux died…' Naomi said.

'Yes.' Barb rolled her eyes. 'We'd have lasted five minutes otherwise. She went through staff like a dose of salts.' Barb had started to chat more easily with Naomi now and had admitted that all the staff had no idea, apart from what they read, how serious Jobe's illness was. 'Twenty-five years we've been here now. Bernard's worried that we won't get another live-in job if…' She paused. 'Well, there's nothing to be gained stressing about that.'

It was clear to Naomi that she was stressing, though.

Naomi's little ploy to keep Ava awake and Merida asleep seemed to have worked. After a bath and dressed in her little sleepsuit, Ava was more than ready to feed and Merida seemed a lot more relaxed.

'What time will Ethan be back?' Naomi asked as Ava fed.

'He just called, he's going to come and have some dinner and then head over to the hospital. They're meeting with Jobe and his specialist. He's not doing so well. The treatment he's having just drains him. It's tough. Especially as Ethan and he have just started talking. I mean really talking.'

'You said they'd just started to get on. Weren't they close before?'

'No.' Merida shook her head. 'Oh, they worked together and were polite and everything but Ethan grew up thinking that his father had had an affair with his nanny and that was the reason that their mother had left…' Merida took a breath. 'This is just between us?'

'Of course.'

'Their mother was absolutely awful. Everything in the press has her painted as a saint and Jobe let Ethan think that. Over the months I've been piecing things together but finally Jobe confirmed it—she was cruel. The reason Elizabeth left was because Jobe had found out what was going on. She painted herself as the perfect mother but she just ignored the boys. More than that, she neglected them. She left Ethan in a car once, in the height of summer. If Abe hadn't told the nanny his brother was still in the car…' She shook her head. 'Abe nearly drowned in the bath. If the nanny hadn't come in when she had…'

Naomi shuddered.

'Apparently the nanny that everyone thinks Jobe had an affair with was actually the person who stood up for the boys. She told Jobe all that was going on. He'd always been too busy with work but as soon as he knew he confronted Elizabeth. She headed off to the Caribbean, insinuating she'd found out that Jobe was sleeping with the nanny. When she had her accident Jobe's name was mud, but he never revealed the truth, not even to Ethan, until the night Ava was born.'

‘What about Abe?’ Naomi asked. ‘Did he think his father had cheated?’

‘No.’ Merida shook her head. ‘Apparently he always knew that the mother was awful. He always looked out for Ethan. Hard to believe, really, when he never gives Ava a glance. But who knows what he went through? Perhaps that’s why he’s so dark. He was never under the illusion that his mother was perfect, far from it. Jobe put up with a lot from the press and, sure, he’s had his fair share of wives and drama, but he’s done his best as a father.’

‘Do you think he’ll make it till Christmas?’

‘I don’t know,’ Merida said. ‘There’s the big ball on Christmas Eve and Jobe insists that it goes ahead. I can’t imagine going.’

‘It’s still a couple of weeks away.’

‘It’s ten days away.’ Merida grimaced. ‘I haven’t a hope of getting into a dress. I’m rather hoping that Abe and Candice can fly the Devereux flag without us.’

Naomi felt her cheeks go warm from the sting of Merida’s words, but thankfully her friend carried on chatting away and didn’t notice. ‘Khalid’s flying in on Friday and Ethan’s meeting him for dinner and things. It’s all business as usual, except we all know that it’s not…’

Naomi wondered if she should tell Merida that the staff were worried too but decided against it. She certainly didn’t want to add to Merida’s stress, especially when finally both mother and baby looked more relaxed.

'She's asleep.' Merida smiled.

'And she took a good feed.'

'I don't know how I'd have done this without you,' Merida admitted.

'I've hardly done anything. You've had her in with you at night.'

'Honestly, you've been amazing, Naomi. I was all set to put her on the bottle this morning.'

'She's a fussy little thing.' Naomi smiled. 'I think if you can stretch her out again, especially with Ethan being out tonight, then you might get her into a bit more of a routine. Let me have her and I'll bring her up to you again at ten and then again at two.'

'You'll be exhausted.'

'That's what you're paying me to be,' Naomi pointed out, but that didn't work with Merida, so she changed tack. 'I can sleep tomorrow,' Naomi said with a smile. 'This is like a holiday for me, Merida. Usually I have the baby, or babies, twenty-four seven and just take them in to the mother for feeding and cuddles and such.'

'Well, it's great that you're here.' She looked down at her now contented baby.

'Then use me.'

Merida looked up. 'Ethan wanted me to go for dinner with Khalid on Friday. He's hoping to soothe the feathers that Abe's ruffled.'

'Is there still no agreement?'

'None. Abe refuses to budge.'

'Why don't you go?' Naomi suggested. 'Dinner sounds far less daunting than a ball and you know that I'll babysit.'

'I don't really want to go,' Merida said. 'And I don't need you to babysit. I thought might go to the hotel and take Ava. Just have a nice night away...'

'Sounds perfect,' Naomi said. 'And even better if we can get her sleeping between feeds.'

'Would you be okay, though?'

'I'm sure I can find something to do,' Naomi teased—they were in New York after all. 'Go!'

It was a plan, and all the more reason to get little Ava settled, so for this night at least Naomi assumed more of a nanny role. When Ava woke up half an hour later, again Naomi walked the floor and did the same thing at ten. 'I'll take her downstairs,' Naomi said, because her little cries wafted from Naomi's floor right up to Merida's. 'And I'll bring her back for another feed at two. She is sleeping more in between, Merida,' Naomi assured the new mother. 'And she's taking much bigger feeds now.'

And so at midnight Naomi sat in the drawing room, holding a still wakeful Ava, although she wasn't crying now. Just alert and awake and utterly gorgeous.

'You *are* going to sleep after the next feed,' Naomi told her. 'And you're going to be good for your mummy on Friday night…' Her one-sided chatter stilled as the door opened. Ava must have picked up on Naomi's sudden tension because she started to cry.

And Naomi was tense because almost two weeks after she'd seen him last, Abe was finally here. Until now she had only seen him in a suit or coat, but tonight he wore black jeans and a thin black jumper, his immaculate hair needed a cut and he was unshaven. He looked like he could be on a wanted poster, Naomi thought.

He most certainly was.

Wanted.

Not that she dared to show it.

'Hey.' He gave her a grim smile as he came into the drawing room. 'I wasn't expecting anyone to be up.'

'I was just about to take Ava upstairs.'

'No need, I'm heading up myself.'

'Then I'll stay down here,' Naomi said, and then, worried he'd think she meant she was avoiding him, added, 'I mean, I'm trying to get her into a routine, she'd only disturb you.'

'I don't think anything would disturb me tonight. Do you want one…?' he offered as he poured himself a drink.

'No, thank you.'

As he poured, Naomi sneaked a look and what she saw concerned her. He'd lost weight—his trousers hung lower on his hips and he looked utterly exhausted. There were dark smudges under his eyes, and the fan of lines looked deeper than they had just a short while ago.

'How's Jobe?'

Abe didn't answer at first but not because he was ignoring her. It was more that he had to dig deep to find a steady voice.

'He's just made the decision to stop all treatments.' It was the first time he'd said it out loud. So badly had he wanted to dissuade his father, to suggest he try to stay for Christmas, or make it to the New Year. Yet he'd known deep down he was being selfish. He was used to making decisions and it was terribly hard to accept that this one wasn't his.

'I'm so sorry.'

Abe took a belt of his drink and let out a long-held breath. 'He says he wants to enjoy the time he has left, and the meds are making him tired and nauseous. He used to love his food.'

'He might again,' Naomi offered.

'That's what he's hoping.' Abe nodded. 'Ethan's staying there tonight. I was going to go home but then I remembered I'm minus a driver.'

'How come?'

'He's moving to Florida.'

'Oh.'

'The snow's really piling up. I don't want to be too far away just in case.'

'Abe...' Naomi knew, even if it was awkward, that she had to broach things. Jobe's health trumped a moment spent blushing. 'I would hate to think you might be staying away because of me...'

'Of course not.'

He had been, though.

It had been one day, he kept telling himself.

No big deal.

Yet it had been the nicest day he had known.

And her company still was.

So much so that despite his intention to head straight up to bed, instead he sat down and looked over at little Ava. 'How is she?'

'Being difficult in the way two-week-old babies generally are. Don't catch her eyes. She's looking for attention when she should be sleeping. We're trying to get her into a routine.'

'Maybe she's like her uncle and loathes routine.'

'Well, she's certainly been burning the candle at both ends.'

Instantly Naomi regretted her words for they seeped the indignation she felt and they told him, if he listened closely, that she'd been reading up on his rather wild ways.

But there was no retrieving them so she just screwed her eyes closed for a second and then prised them open and stared into the fire and offered an apology.

'That sounded...' She didn't know what to say.

'No wonder you've been avoiding home. All I need is a rolling pin and to be standing at the door.'

He gave a low laugh, taken aback by her honesty, so he returned it.

'I *have* been avoiding coming here,' he admitted. 'Not because I didn't want to see you, more because I did.'

Her eyes filled with tears, and she felt her face redden—or was it the glow of the fire?—but in that midnight hour it felt as if there was space to be honest, and admit to the hurt she'd felt. 'I know it was just a kiss to you, Abe, but it was my first.'

She didn't look at his reaction, didn't want to see the surprise on his face. Yet there wasn't any. At some level, he'd known that the mouth that had met his had been an inexperienced one, that the woman he had held in his arm had not flown into them easily, and the hurt he had caused gnawed at his gut.

'You shouldn't have wasted it on me,' Abe said in a deep, low voice that both scalded and soothed her soul.

'It wasn't wasted.'

There wasn't silence between them, just little noises from Ava as she tried to catch an adult's eye in the hope of staying awake awhile. And it was Abe who gave in to her, taking one of her little hands and watching as the tiny fingers coiled around his.

Naomi didn't halt him, or warn him that he was messing up a routine. Some things were important and to see him care for his niece, to reach out and get to know her, felt as if a small battle had been won.

And he wanted to warn Naomi, to tell her to stay the hell away, yet he moved closer, not physically but sitting beside her felt so right it reminded him of just how wrong the world could be.

'When Ethan was born, we had a family photo taken,' Abe said, 'sitting on this sofa. And then Jobe and I headed up to the terrace garden for some father-son shots. It was for a magazine.'

'How old were you?'

'Four,' Abe said, 'nearly five.'

And she smiled because on that glorious day they'd shared, he'd told her things about his father. About pizzas and pretzels, and precious times spent.

'I came back down. I think I'd forgotten something and I found Ethan lying face down on the sofa…'

The smile drained from her face.

'Like one of the cushions. Elaine, the nanny, came in and I remember her turning him over and he was purple. She was shouting at me for not picking him up, for not doing something…'

'Where was your mother?'

'She'd gone for a lie down. Just dropped him like a doll once the photo was over. I never let him out of my sight after that. I used to dread coming home from school, wondering if he'd be safe. It's hard to believe that he's now a father himself.'

'And a very good one.'

'Yes.'

He didn't know if Naomi knew about the contract between him and Merida. It seemed irrelevant now. Abe could see how happy his brother and Merida were and, like every new father, Ethan came in every day with tales about his new baby.

And his wife.

Despite the contract and Abe's gloomy predictions, it would seem they were very much in love.

It made his relationship with Candice, or rather the lack of it, so hollow.

So shallow.

Or rather, more simply, low.

And as Abe looked down at the fingers so tightly holding his, he knew that the woman who held this baby deserved to know that her first kiss hadn't been entirely wasted on a cheat.

Even if it broke the terms of a contract he himself was bound to.

'Naomi, I can't really go into details but I am sorry that I wasn't upfront with you about Candice.'

'It doesn't matter.' She shook her head, loath to confront things.

'I think that it does.'

Naomi swallowed. She just looked at down at Ava, who lay blowing bubbles and utterly content and oblivious to a sometimes cruel world.

'This can't go any further,' Abe said.

'She's two weeks old.' Naomi deliberately misinterpreted, deflecting with a tease, but then she was serious. 'If you mean me, you don't have to worry, I'd never breathe a word.'

'I know that.' Intrinsically he did. 'The truth is that Candice and I have an arrangement—as far as the press and the board are concerned, we're in a relationship. We're not, though.'

Naomi frowned, she simply didn't understand. 'But she came to the hospital to visit Ava, you're going to the Devereux ball together…' she pointed out, recalling Merida's words.

'It's for appearances' sake,' Abe said. 'The ball is just work and I have to take someone.'

'So it's just an act?'

He nodded, but that wasn't enough for Naomi.

'Are you saying that you've never been in a relationship and that you've never slept with her?'

'No. We were together for a while. What I'm saying is that lately we haven't been. We don't…'

'And she doesn't have feelings for you?' Naomi did look at him then, and she watched his jaw clamp down. 'If you offered her more, she wouldn't take it?'

'It's not like that,' he insisted. 'We have an agreement.'

But Naomi had heard enough. 'Abe,' she said, 'can we not do this?'

'But I want to tell you how it is.'

'Well, I really don't want to hear it.'

'Naomi...'

'Please, Abe, we're both very different. Thank you for trying to explain things to me, and I'm glad that you don't think you were cheating.'

'I wasn't.'

Her eyes told him she believed otherwise.

'Look, I believe you when you say that you have arrangements in place and all sorts, but it sounds like a recipe for hurt to me. And I would never knowingly hurt someone. It's a promise I made to myself a long time ago.' She looked right at him. 'I could have so easily gone the other way, Abe.' She never did the woe is me with her childhood, but she opened a tiny window on it then.

'I was moved from pillar to post and some of those pillars and posts weren't very nice. I was so close to sticking my fingers up at the world. I was so close to going off the rails but instead of being nasty, I chose to be kind. And, as much as I want to, I can't really believe that Candice is okay with it all.'

'Naomi, she is. I pay for her apartment and—'

'Abe, I don't want to hear it. We had a wonderful day out and we shared a kiss at the end...' She tried to downplay it, to somehow neatly file it away. 'Let's not make it any more complicated than that.'

'It doesn't have to be.' His voice dropped to huskiness and his eyes were as black and as enticing as treacle. A personal preference perhaps, but treacle was up there with her favourite things. Yet more dangerous than a sugar hit was the pull of Abe, and how she had to fight not to lean into him.

To forgive and forget, or at least pretend to.

Thank goodness for Ava, Naomi thought, for without her she might just have given in, but instead she gave a slight shake of her head, as if to clear the spell. 'Please, Abe.' She just came out and said it. 'It might be completely straightforward to you but it's all just too sordid for me.'

He just sat there as, without malice, she gave her verdict.

She was close to tears and didn't want him to see them, or to resume this conversation, so she chose to make a rapid escape. 'Could you hold Ava for me, please?'

'Sorry?' Abe said, his mind miles away.

Her words had been like a punch to the gut, but he didn't show that, of course.

'I need the loo and if I put her down now she'll just start crying.'

He hadn't held Ava.

Not once.

He held out his arms and when Naomi handed her over, she was so tiny and light that it felt as if he was catching air.

And Naomi disappeared and left him, literally, holding the baby.

Such a new baby.

And he knew that Ava would be okay.

Abe had spent his early years looking out for his brother, and the later years protecting Ethan's false image of his mother.

He must have got something right, Abe decided, for it would seem Ethan was far more capable of love than he.

Naomi's summing up hung in the air.

Sordid.

Abe had never looked at his life from the outside before and until then he had never really cared what others thought.

Yet he found himself caring what Naomi thought.

If she'd just let him explain…

He and Candice had come to an arrangement a long time ago, when they had first broken up.

Or rather when he had ended things.

He thought back to Candice's pleading and pointing out the anger emanating from the board about his reckless ways. It had been Candice who had suggested that they lie and pretend that they were back together. If she could appear to have forgiven him, then surely the rest would follow?

It had worked.

For eighteen months there had been a veneer of respectability.

Sure, he had been *caught* at times, but with each passing affair Candice had provided an air of stability.

Yes, despite his attempts to justify things, Abe looked down at his niece and thought about Naomi's question on the night she'd been born.

What sort of uncle do you want to be?

Not this one.

And as Abe searched the depths of his soul, Naomi looked into the bathroom mirror and asked a similar question of herself, about the type of woman she was.

Oh, she wanted to believe Abe—that it was all neat and straightforward and that there was really nothing untoward about the kiss they had shared. Yes, Naomi wanted to believe him because, quite simply, she would like more time in his arms.

She would like to go back in there now and say that she had the night off on Friday. That perhaps they could go and see the Christmas lights. That they could possibly continue from where they had left off.

But she'd meant what she'd said—his arrangement with Candice was too sordid for her.

So she splashed water on her face and then dried off and blew out a long breath before heading back to the drawing room, where she paused at the door. Little Ava was finally asleep in Abe's arms and when she approached, Abe looked up, gave a small smile and with his free hand put a finger to his lips.

'You got her to sleep.'

'Isn't that what babies do?' Abe asked.

'Not this one. I thought she'd be awake till two. I might even get an hour's sleep.'

'Are you taking her up to Merida?'

'No, Ava's in with me tonight.' She held out her arms but as Abe went to pass her across little Ava's little face frowned at the intrusion.

'I'll carry her up.'

They headed up the stairs and into Naomi's suite, where there was a crib set up for little Ava. He placed her in it very tenderly and pulled the little sheet over her with great care.

And then he turned and faced Naomi.

She wanted to fall into his arms. It felt as if there was an iron bar attempting to unbuckle her knees so she might just topple onto him.

And if she did, he would catch her.

He would hold her and he would kiss her and it wasn't some sense of professionalism that stopped her, for he would take her from here and lead her to the bedroom.

They wanted each other.

As inexperienced as she was, that much she knew.

And it wasn't just the thought of Candice that held her back.

He melted her with his eyes, he turned her world and spun it gold, and she could not fathom untangling herself from him.

There could be no dusting herself off and carrying on when he inevitably ended things.

And it would be he who ended them, Naomi was sure. And if his internet history was anything to go by, she'd be nursing a broken heart this side of the New Year, and she was supposed to be in New York until the end of January.

Oh, get out now, she told herself.

With one kiss, she was already in way too deep.

And so, instead of leaning into him, as her body instructed, she gave him a smile.

'Thanks,' she said in an upbeat voice, as if he was Barb and had just popped into her room and dropped off a pile of Ava's washing.

'No problem,' he said, as if he'd done the same. ''Night, then.'

''Night, Abe.'

It was better this way.

Surely?

CHAPTER SIX

THERE WERE NO further sightings of Abe.

Ava woke at two, and she could see the light coming from a room down the hall.

When she woke at six and she carried little Ava toward the stairs, Naomi caught a hit of his cologne, the clear, sharp scent of bergamot, and she knew, simply knew, he had showered and left.

And she knew, just knew, he would not be staying tonight.

She should be relieved, Naomi told herself, yet she felt anything but as she lay the next night, awaiting a creak on the stairs that might indicate he'd come home.

It never came.

Friday dawned.

Her official day off, and when she came down to the kitchen Barb told her she should have stayed in bed. 'I was going to bring you up breakfast. I used to do it in the old days on the nanny's day off.'

'I don't eat breakfast,' Naomi reminded Barb, at

the very same time that she selected a pastry and they shared a smile. They both knew she'd lied.

'You can have breakfast in bed for your birthday,' Barb said, refusing to be put off. 'Merida said it's coming up. I'll make you my special.'

'What's your special?' Naomi asked, licking her lips. 'I am dying to try lox.'

'Do you value your kidneys?' Barb checked, and Naomi laughed.

'I love salt.'

'Hmm.' Barb wasn't so sure. 'You'll have to get yourself dinner tonight, given it's the staff Christmas party. You should come,' Barb pushed, for she'd asked her before. 'It's at Barnaby's. Jobe takes his household staff there every year. Usually he's with us, of course.' She cast an anxious look at Naomi. 'Have you heard how he is?'

'Not really,' Naomi fudged, and she truly felt torn. Abe had told her that Jobe had stopped all treatment, though that had been a very personal conversation. It was one of the reasons she had declined the offer to go tonight. She knew they might press her for more information and she didn't think it was her place to share information. 'I know he's been off his food.'

'We all know that!' Uncharacteristically Barb snapped. 'I'm sorry,' she said quickly. 'It's just hell, not knowing. I pick up snatches of conversation but, of course, no one thinks to tell us.'

Merida came in then, her red hair freshly washed

and looking a whole lot more like her old self. Barb snapped back into housekeeper mode, asking what time their luggage would be ready to take to the hotel.

'Ethan's going to meet me at the hotel,' Merida said. 'I should be ready to leave by five. Does that give you time to get ready for your party?'

'Of course.' Barb nodded but, Naomi noted, she didn't ask Merida if there was any news on Jobe.

It was a lovely day, cold and brisk. They bundled Ava up and headed out to a café and had spiced Christmas coffees, just two friends sharing a gorgeous day out.

'I thought you wanted to do the river cruise on your day off,' Merida checked.

'I'm going to do it after Christmas,' Naomi said, slathering butter on a slab of warm gingerbread. 'Are you looking forward to going away tonight?'

'I am.' Merida grinned. 'Though I'm not so sure that Ethan is, given that he's got to deal with the daggers flying between Abe and Khalid.'

'Oh, is Abe going?' Naomi asked, oh, so casually.

'Apparently. They're meeting at the office beforehand and then heading from there to dinner. I'm so glad that I'm not expected to join them. Ava and I shall be watching the movie channel.'

Naomi laughed.

From all Naomi could glean, Abe had stood firm and refused to give in to demands, although construction had not ceased, as had been threatened by Khalid.

'You *can* leave her with me,' Naomi reminded Merida, while mentally crossing her fingers that Merida wouldn't because, determined not to dwell on Abe, she had made plans for tonight. Still, she would cancel her plans if need be, but thankfully Merida declined.

'I know you'll have her, but I really want to see how I go without back-up,' Merida said with a smile. 'You're welcome to come. Ethan can book you a room…'

'I am *not* coming on your date night,' Naomi said.

'It's hardly a date night. I just hope Ethan can smooth things over with Khalid. Abe's just about jeopardised the whole project,' Merida said. 'He should have discussed this with Ethan at the time rather than shutting down talks.'

'Oh, so he should have popped his head around the door while you were giving birth?' Naomi didn't really have a clue what the issues were but she couldn't help but jump to Abe's defence.

'I guess.' Merida rolled her eyes. 'You won't come?'

'No.'

'So, what are you going to do tonight? You'll have the place to yourself as it's the staff Christmas dinner.'

'I know…' Naomi hesitated, wondering if she should broach the subject of just how worried the staff all were about Jobe, but she knew it didn't come down to Merida to tell them, and so she carried on chatting instead. 'Barb asked if I wanted to go with them, but I thought I might take in a Broadway show.'

'Do you know what you want to see? I can sort out tickets…'

As an actress *and* a Devereux, no doubt Merida wouldn't have a problem securing plum seats even this close to Christmas, but Naomi had already sorted it out, though she was hesitant to admit it, worried that it might upset Merida. 'I've already got a ticket.'

'For what?' Merida asked, then must have seen Naomi blush. 'You're going to see *Night Forest*, aren't you?'

'Yes, it's just I've heard so much from you about it that I wanted to see it for myself. I didn't think I had a hope of getting a ticket, but it would seem one ticket is easier to get at the last minute. You're not upset?' Naomi checked, because she knew it had broken Merida's heart to step away from playing Belladonna.

'I would have been upset a short while ago,' Merida admitted. 'Not that you were going, more at the very mention of its name. But not now.' She did up the last of the poppers on Ava's outfit and scooped her up for a kiss. 'Ava more than makes up for it. And, anyway, it doesn't have to spell the end of my career. Ethan and I have spoken and I'm going to see if I can go back when Ava's a little bit older. Maybe as an understudy.'

'Part time?'

Merida nodded. 'It's far too soon to be thinking of it now, but it's nice that Ethan's been so encouraging.'

It was odd, but it was at moments like this that Naomi felt lonely.

And it wasn't about Merida and Ethan being happy, or pining for Abe—in fact, it had nothing to do with coupledom. It was about families, and having support and someone completely in your corner.

It was all the things that Naomi had missed.

Not that she showed it, or said anything. Instead, it was Merida who spoke. 'I'm actually pleased that you're going to see it. Sabine, my old understudy, is now Belladonna. I'd love to hear what you think. Ethan has been twice and so far only gotten to see one half of it…' The first time Ethan had gone had been opening night when, thanks to her absence on stage, he had found out that Merida was pregnant.

The second time had been when he'd taken Merida and she had gone into labour.

'Well,' Naomi said, 'I intend to see the whole thing and I'll let you know what I think tomorrow.'

The day passed in a blur and if Naomi had been in any doubt as to the status of Ethan and Merida's relationship when she'd first arrived, it was completely put to rest when Ethan unexpectedly arrived home to take his wife and daughter on their first night out.

He was so gorgeous to both Merida and little Ava that it made Naomi's heart twist to see the little family so happy as they headed off for their first trip away.

Even though Naomi wasn't a new mother, she ran on the same timeline as one. Worse, because she'd spent most of the afternoon helping Merida get ready, there was little time to do the same for herself. So by the time Merida had gone there wasn't time for Naomi to wash her hair so she just had a quick shower and then tackled her limited wardrobe.

For the most part her clothes were practical for work and, given the transitory nature of her work, there wasn't much going out at night. She had two nice dresses. One that she usually wore for christenings and things but it was far too summery. The other was black and gorgeous but she had put on even more weight since she'd last worn it and her cleavage spilled out.

It would just have to do, she decided. She'd be wearing her new red coat there and for inside the theatre she had a lovely silver scarf.

Naomi applied her make-up carefully, put on her not so little black dress and told herself to smile when she looked in the mirror. After all, on her night off she was going to see *Night Forest* on Broadway!

And, of course, she was excited.

Well, not really.

But she didn't want, even to herself, to admit that.

There had been a dull ache, or rather a space in her chest, since the other night. A space that Naomi did not want to examine because if she did she might break down and cry.

It was just a kiss.

She kept saying that like a mantra.

But Abe's was the only kiss she had ever known, and worse, far worse, was the feeling she had let both of them down the other night. He'd tried to talk but she'd felt unable to listen.

As she headed downstairs the staff were all getting ready to pile into the cars lined up in the drive for them.

'You look wonderful,' Naomi said to Barb.

'I could say the same for you. It feels odd to be heading to the party without Jobe. Maybe next year.'

Naomi said nothing.

It was hell sometimes, having a foot both upstairs and down, but surely the staff ought to know?

When they had gone, Naomi went to order a car of her own. The staff phone was ringing in the kitchen but she ignored it. After all, it couldn't be for her.

As she went to get her coat from the cloakroom, it reminded her so much of her day with Abe that she just buried her face in it for a long moment. There was the faintest scent of him, she was sure. Naomi didn't wear perfume and there was a sharp, clean note of bergamot on the collar. And she recognised another, wood sage, she was sure. It was the scent she had breathed in when they had kissed. The same scent that had met her in the hallway the morning he had left before dawn.

Then the phone rang again and she suddenly thought of Jobe and how sick he was and decided she ought to pick it up.

'Devereux household.'

'Naomi?'

She closed her eyes at the sound of Abe's voice.

Not for a second did she think it might be Ethan, even if they spoke with the same accent, even if their voices were both deep and low. It was as if Abe's were etched like a signature on her heart.

'Yes.'

'Is Barb there?'

'It's the staff dinner tonight,' Naomi reminded him. 'Everybody's out.'

'Of course.' He let out a sigh. 'It doesn't matter.'

'Is everything okay?' she couldn't help but ask. 'Is Jobe—?'

'He's good,' Abe said quickly, as he hadn't intended to alarm her. 'Well, when I say good, now that he's off a lot of the meds he's suddenly hungry and eating.' He spoke so easily with her. 'As well as that he's talking. A lot. Reminiscing, I guess.'

'I thought…' She hesitated. As far as she knew, Abe was supposed to be out with Ethan and Khalid tonight, but it would seem he'd chosen to spend the time with his father. It wasn't her place to pry.

'There's a photo he wants. I was going to ask Barb if she could take it down and have Bernard bring it over...'

'I can do that.'

'Would you?'

'Of course. Where's the photo?'

'It's on the main staircase,' Abe said, and he could hear the clip of her heels as she walked on the marble floor of the entrance. 'Are you on your way out?'

'Why?'

'I can hear heels.'

'Yes, I'm on my way out.' Naomi offered no more information than that.

'Where are you going?'

'Why?'

'I'm just curious.'

He could remain so, Naomi decided. 'I'm at the stairs.'

'Okay, about a third of the way up there's a photo of Ethan and me eating pizza...'

'There's one of the two of you on a yacht, and there's one of you...'

She was looking through his youth.

There were load of formal shots and then she saw the one he had referred to the other night. Ethan was a tiny baby and Abe was sitting on his father's knee, wearing a smile. Elizabeth was looking adoringly at the newborn she held.

And this was one picture, Naomi thought, that didn't paint a thousand words—instead it lied.

Only not quite, because now that she knew Abe she could see the fixed smile and that it did not meet his eyes.

'It's halfway up the stairs,' Abe said, trying to direct her, and Naomi dragged her eyes away and located the correct photo.

'Got it.'

It was gorgeous. Abe was looking very serious but more relaxed than in the others, and Ethan was holding a huge slice of pizza. Jobe was squinting against the sun that shone in his eyes.

'I'll bring it over now,' Naomi said.

'Are you sure you don't mind? I can wait outside if there's somewhere you need to be…' he fished shamelessly. 'I mean if you have a reservation or you're meeting someone.'

'It's really no problem,' Naomi said, and carried on being evasive. She wasn't bitchy in the least but she did manage a rather satisfied smile when she ended the call, because he clearly wanted to know what she was up to tonight.

Well, Abe Devereux could keep right on guessing.

Naomi was actually well ahead of time as she left the house. She'd allowed ages for the snow but, of course, New York was considerably more geared up for heavy snowfall than London, and her ride soon arrived.

As she climbed into the car, though, instead of asking to be taken to the private wing of the hospital, Naomi thought of what Abe had said about his father eating and him being rarely hungry, and she made a decision.

'Could we take a little detour on the way to the hospital?' Naomi asked. 'I want to get a pretzel.'

'From?' the driver asked.

'The first cart we see.'

It didn't take long to find one and before long she arrived at Jobe's door. For Abe it was like a breath of fresh air had swept in. Hospital visits, even the better ones, were hard going at times and she just breezed in wearing her red coat and her hair glossy, and for the first time he saw her made up. But it was her smile and her effortless way with his father that knocked him sideways.

'Hi, there, Jobe.' Naomi smiled and went straight over. 'It's Naomi, Ava's nanny and Merida's friend...' He gave a nod of recognition. 'It's so good to see you again.'

'Am I already in heaven?' he asked. 'What's that smell?'

'I brought in a pretzel.'

And whether he could eat it or not, it didn't matter. The scent alone made him smile.

'Where are you off to?' Jobe asked.

'It's a secret,' Abe answered for her. 'We're not allowed to ask.'

And then he looked at Naomi as her face broke into a smile. They had been teasing and flirting, even if she refused to admit it.

'Jobe can know,' Naomi said. 'I'm going to see *Night Forest*. The production your daughter-in-law—'

'I've seen it,' Jobe said. 'You're in for a magical night. Who's the lucky fellow?'

'Jobe, I've barely been in the country for three weeks! And,' she added, 'I'm working.'

'Not tonight you're not,' Jobe said, taking in her heels and make-up. 'Where are Ethan and Merida?'

'They're out with Khalid,' Abe said. 'I chose to give it a miss, though I can feel my ears burning.'

'You took a risk,' Jobe scolded.

'Someone had to.' Abe shrugged.

'Well, you should have spoken to me about it,' Jobe insisted. 'Not that he's ever come to me for advice,' he added, rolling his eyes for Naomi's benefit, and that made her giggle. And that made Jobe smile. 'You know, while you're here you should go to the Devereux Christmas Eve Ball. It's the best night of the year.'

'I'm working.'

'Pah!' Jobe said. 'I thought Merida said that she didn't want a nanny.' Jobe looked at his son. 'You could take her. Ethan will be there with Merida...'

'Stop interfering.' Abe's voice was harsh, and it was Naomi's first glimpse of it, not that it seemed to bother Jobe.

'Just saying.'

'Well, don't.'

Naomi looked at Abe's gritted jaw and gave a tight smile. She didn't blame Jobe, of course, he was a little confused and was just being nice, but it made an already awkward situation worse.

'I have to go, Jobe,' Naomi said. 'You look after yourself.'

And when she had safely gone, confused or not, Abe waved a finger at his father. 'Don't even go there.'

'What?'

'Suggesting I take someone to the ball.'

'She's only here for a few weeks, she deserves a big night out…'

'I've never asked for your permission or help with my love life, and I shan't start now.'

'I never said anything about love,' Jobe said. 'I was just saying take the girl to the ball. She's nice.'

Abe said nothing.

'Remember how I used to buy you one of these to warm your hands?' Jobe said.

'Sure.'

'Even back then, you never told me what was on your mind.' He wasn't confused now, just bewildered that Abe hadn't been able to come to him. That he'd had to hear from the nanny what was going on in his own home. 'You could have told me, Abe…'

'I know now.'

'Why didn't you?' Jobe said, and then he gave a wry laugh. 'I know, even back then you trusted no one.'

He stayed a few hours, doing work when his father dozed then making small talk when he woke up.

And then it moved from small talk to more serious matters as Jobe tried to tie the loose ends in his life. 'I don't like this business with Candice.'

'Don't worry about that now.'

'But I do.'

'Well, you don't have to. I ended it this afternoon.'

'How did she take it?'

He should possibly soothe his father and assure him everything was fine, but that would make him a liar. 'Not very well.'

'I don't trust her, Abe.'

'You're a Devereux and, as you just pointed out, we don't trust anyone,' Abe quipped. 'Don't worry about it.'

And Jobe stopped worrying about Candice and lay back on his pillows and saw the foil from his pretzel and he was back to the days of his sons' childhoods again and reminiscing.

'Nice girl,' Jobe said, just before he dozed off again.

'Yes, she is,' he admitted this time.

And for Abe, that was the problem.

She was so nice that now he would never be able to eat a pretzel again without thinking of not just long-ago times with his father but the day he and Naomi had spent, and now the gift she had given him and his father tonight…

The memories both evoked and made.

CHAPTER SEVEN

THAT *NICE GIRL* sat feeling blue and alone in a packed theatre.

Well, not alone. The seat had been available because, after all, few people go to the theatre alone, so Naomi found herself on the end seat beside one huge, happy family, and Naomi listened to their plans for Christmas and New Year. And, yes, this one she'd be spending with her dear friend and the person she was closest to in the world.

Yet it was Merida and Ethan's first family Christmas and Ava's first.

Naomi knew that, no matter how kind and welcoming they were, she'd feel a bit of a spare part.

Oh, Merida would do her best to make sure that Naomi was included but tonight that was how Naomi felt—like a spare part in a two by two, loved-up world.

It was a relief when the lights finally dimmed and she could lose herself in another world.

The production was breath-taking, so much so

that Naomi forgot that the birds were actors, but when Belladonna came on, Naomi knew this had been Merida's part. When she heard Sabine singing and realised the complexity of the role it hit home just how talented and accomplished Merida truly was.

And she was so proud of Merida, but tonight, as she stood next to the very large family for the standing ovation and applauded the cast, Naomi felt very small.

Well, *not*-small Naomi was well aware that she could lose the equivalent weight of three Avas and still have more to go, but tonight she felt insignificant and more than a little alone in this world.

It took for ever to get a cab, and Naomi had to walk for ages until the theatre crowd thinned out. It was cold with an icy wind, which didn't help matters much, and she wasn't assertive enough with her flagging, but finally she was sitting in the back of a warm cab and would soon be home.

The Christmas lights were amazing and the drive was a night-time version of the walk she had taken with Abe.

But this time as they passed the Rockefeller Center she was alone.

And the sight of the lights in the stores along Fifth Avenue reminded her of teardrops and suddenly Naomi let her own fall.

Oh, she loathed feeling sorry for herself, but to-night she did.

It was her own fault, Naomi knew.

She could have been with Abe tonight.

Naomi knew it in her heart.

The right thing to do really was the hardest thing.

But then the nicest thing happened. Whoever had warned her about New York cabbies clearly hadn't met this one, because he was so kind that he handed her a wad of kitchen roll to wipe her eyes.

'Christmas makes it that much harder…' he said.

'It does,' Naomi agreed, and his insight just made her cry some more.

Then he told her about his wife, and how much he missed her, so much so that he chose to work through the nights. He was the nicest cab driver in the world.

'You work for the Devereuxes?' he commented, as they pulled up at the huge grey house.

'I do.' Naomi nodded.

No, it wasn't really home.

Tomorrow she'd put her game face on again.

Just not tonight.

She turned the key and stepped into the entrance and had to think for a moment to remember the code, but then she stood rigid as Abe came up beside her and she watched as his long fingers punched it in.

'You've been crying.'

It sounded more like an accusation. 'No, I'm just cold.'

'It must be the night for it,' Abe said. 'Barb just said the same thing, but in your case I don't believe it has anything to do with the wind chill factor.'

Naomi didn't even bother to take off her coat, she would do that upstairs. She just brushed past him and had made it halfway to the stairs when he spoke.

'I'm sorry,' Abe said. And even though it was his first apology in all his years on this earth, it didn't go down well.

'Sorry for what?' Naomi said, and then spun around.

'Upsetting you,' Abe said. 'For not telling you about Candice.'

'You!' Naomi shouted. 'It's not all about you, Abe.' She was furious, not just with him but with herself, because of course he was there at the bottom of the well she was crying from, not that she'd let him know that. 'You're so arrogant. Doesn't it even enter your head that I might have other things to be crying about?'

Abe just stood there, which was a feat in itself. Usually he turned his back on hysterics or drama, especially when they were of the female kind.

'Christmas is *hard* for some people. Not that you even celebrate it. And, no, Barb wasn't crying because of the wind…' She stopped herself, because it wasn't right to break Barb's confidence in the heat of the moment.

So she collected herself.

'Believe it or not, I wasn't crying about you.' She shot him a look that confirmed it and didn't even bother to say goodnight, just headed up the stairs and closed her door in relief.

Damn Abe for seeing her cry.

She took off her coat and then held in a choice word when there was a knock at the door.

'Naomi?'

'Go away,' she called out.

'I can't do that,' he replied. 'Not without seeing for myself that you're okay.'

The door opened and she stood in her dress and shoes, her face tear-streaked but angry. 'Well, you can see that I am.' Then she looked down at the bottle of champagne and two glasses he was holding. 'I'm not in the mood for celebrating.'

'That's okay,' he said. 'Neither am I.'

Yet he made no move to go.

'Why should I talk to you?' Naomi said.

'Because there's a lot to talk about.'

'I don't want to hear your excuses.'

'Good,' Abe replied, 'because I don't make them.'

He made her smile, albeit it was a watery one. And she did want to hear what he had to say, so she pulled open the door and let him in and they headed through to her small lounge.

Naomi sat on the sofa and watched as he expertly poured two glasses and handed her one. He looked at her shaking hand as she took it, and then at the slight pull of her face as she took a sip and the way she moved away a touch when he sat down on the sofa.

He knew not to dive in too deep straight away so he asked something that had been troubling him since he'd spoken to Barb.

'What's wrong with Barb?'

Naomi swallowed. 'I shouldn't have said anything.'

'Too late for that.'

'Barb's worried, they all are. They really don't know what's happening. And they're sad too, as well as hopeful. She said to me tonight that she hoped Jobe would be able to come with them next year. I know they're just staff to you, but—'

'Firstly,' Abe said, 'they're my father's staff.'

'I know.'

'When Jobe went into the hospital it was for further treatment. It's only been a few days since he's accepted that it's terminal.' Abe was silent for a moment. 'I haven't.'

Naomi swallowed and suddenly felt terribly small.

Well, not thin and interesting, but she'd just shrunk inside at her own insensitivity.

'I'm starting to, though,' Abe admitted. 'I want him to fight.'

'It must be so hard to let him go.'

Abe nodded. 'I always thought we'd have more time to sort things out…' He didn't elaborate, didn't feel the need to, because it felt as if she understood.

He dragged his mind back to what the conversation was about. 'I will speak to them,' Abe said. 'Stupidly, I thought it might be better to wait until after Christmas…'

'I'm sorry,' Naomi said. 'I shouldn't have said anything.'

'No, I'm very glad that you did. Leave that with me.'

She nodded, rather hoping that their little talk was over. 'Thanks,' she said, and stupidly went to stand.

To see him out.

To say goodbye.

But he took he wrist and pulled her back down onto the couch. 'Why were you crying?'

'I already told you,' she said, and pulled back her arm.

'No…' He dismissed her excuse. 'I think it was a bit more than Bernard and Barb, and you've made it very clear your tears have nothing to do with me. So why were you crying?'

'Why do you care?'

'I'm not sure,' he admitted. 'But I do.'

And so she answered in part. 'Because I'll never be on Broadway.'

'Not you as well,' he groaned. 'I thought that was Merida's beef.'

'No.' Even in the midst of her tears he still made her smile. 'It's more that I could never be. The only real talent that I've got is putting babies to sleep.'

'There are an awful lot of new mothers who would kill for your skills, although, for what it's worth, I think there's an awful lot more to you than that.'

'There really isn't.'

'How about that you go into people's homes at presumably a tumultuous time and make everyone's lives that much better? You certainly have here.'

'Thank you.' She didn't know what to say now. 'I think I'm just tired.'

'Of course you are,' Abe said. 'Getting up to other people's babies every damn night.'

'It's my job to do so, and I happen to love my work, though it has been a busy year,' Naomi admitted. 'I took on an extra client in the summer when I should have taken time off, but it was her second child and I'd been there for the first. And then there were twins before Ava, but the mother delivered early. I just haven't had a break. I'm sure that I'll be fine in a few weeks. I'm taking a decent slice of time off after this,' Naomi said.

'How long?'

'I actually haven't lined up another job. Deliberately.' She had told no one her plans. In fact, 'plans' sounded a rather too grand a word for the tentative ideas that had been taking shape, but he was such bliss to speak to. He just topped up her glass and it felt as if he stopped the clocks too, for time ceased to matter when Abe was around. 'I think it's time to find somewhere more permanent to live. And, when I do, maybe work more locally…' She shook her head. 'I'm not sure. I just want…' She didn't finish or she'd start crying again, but both knew she just wanted a home. 'I don't know where to start looking, though,' Naomi admitted. 'I've lived in so many places.'

'You'll know it when you see it,' Abe said. 'I had an apartment, not far from here. In fact…' He hesitated. It was actually the apartment Candice was in now, but they had never lived there together and it truly wasn't relevant here. 'I still have it, it's on Madison.'

'Nice,' Merida said.

'Perhaps, but it also happens to be ten minutes from my father's and about five minutes from work…' He didn't know how best to explain how confined he'd felt by the exclusive address and the old money vibe of the Upper East Side. 'I just wanted away. I came across this old brownstone in Greenwich Village and I knew straight away that it was where I wanted to live, though when Jobe got wind of it you'd have thought I was moving out to the slums.'

Naomi laughed.

'I just needed a space that wasn't linked to the Devereux name. And a place that was mine. It's more laid back compared to here,' he explained. 'Jobe said I was buying a pile of trouble and admittedly the renovations took a while…'

'You did them?'

'Hell, no, but when I walk in that door I know I'm home. You need that.'

She nodded.

And they weren't talking about fancy addresses, there was no need to clarify that.

'I go to buy something,' Naomi said, 'and I have to think if it will fit in my case, or if I'll have to put it in storage.'

'No more,' he said, and she nodded, relieved to have voiced it, and relieved that she had finally voiced her other thoughts.

'How did you meet Merida?' Abe asked. 'Was it when you shared a flat?'

'No, we were at the same school for a year,' Naomi said. 'I was moved on, but we kept in touch. She wanted to be an actress and I wanted to be a paediatric nurse but the teacher said we were both dreaming.'

'Why?' He frowned. 'I get they might say that about acting...'

'I was very behind at school,' Naomi said. 'I was never going to make the grades to get into nursing.'

'It doesn't sound as if you had the most stable schooling.'

'You make me sound like a horse.' She aimed for a smile but he refused to allow her to joke her way out of it.

'Listen.' He took her face in his hands and his thumbs brushed at the tears but they kept spilling again. It felt to her as if he had tapped a river, it felt as if all the hurt she held inside he *allowed* to come out. And where most ran from raw emotion, he fostered it. 'I'm sure that if a nurse is what you want to be then you could do it.'

Still held by his hands, she shook her head, because she didn't want to be a nurse any more.

'I don't know what I want,' Naomi admitted.

Except that wasn't quite true, because right here, right now she wanted his kiss.

Was it him she wanted, Naomi briefly wondered, or just contact?

And when she met his eyes the answer was simple.

Him.

Yet even when it was held by his hands she shook her head and he knew that she was thinking about Candice.

'We broke up.'

'Abe?' Naomi wanted to believe him, and to her shame she was so hollowed out with want that she almost didn't care, yet she needed more if she was to believe him.

'It's over,' he said. 'I told her yesterday and my father tonight.'

And it was enough clarification, enough that she bent her own rules.

He first kissed her cheek and she closed her eyes at the bliss of contact. His mouth was soft and the room felt very still as he held her so steady. Then she tasted her own tears on his lips as his mouth softly brushed them. It was a kiss that made things better, even if in the morning it might just have made things a whole lot worse.

His tongue slipped in and was met by hers as they toyed with each other. It was a kiss that made her burn and a kiss that somehow soothed. She felt a connection like she never could have envisaged. His scent was faint-inducing, and there was the bergamot, and the wood sage, and now she inhaled a juniper note, and she felt she knew him more now.

His hands left her face but the contact remained as his mouth dizzied her. She felt the cool of the air on her back and it registered that he had pulled down her zip, then she felt the warmth of his palm on her back.

Abe wanted her in bed, yet he made no move to stand because he wanted to kiss her some more.

For Abe, nights necking on a sofa had never happened, let alone were long gone, but he was pulling her dress down over her arms, desperate just to feel her.

'Abe…' She wasn't protesting, but before his kiss toppled her she wanted access to skin and she was pleasingly un-shy and unabashed as he undid her bra, for she was too busy working on the buttons of his shirt.

The crush of him against her chest was delicious. The force of his kiss was denied to her mouth and

Naomi closed her eyes as his mouth tasted her breast, wetting and teasing one nipple and then blowing it cold, and when she ached for more of this pleasure he came back to her mouth.

She never let herself get out of hand, but she let him take her to that place now. His kiss pressed her back onto the sofa and the weight of him atop her was sublime.

He looked down at her, and he wanted her stripped beneath him, but he could not resist one more taste so he kissed her again, a deep, sexy kiss as his hips pressed in.

Her hand pushed at his shirt, and finally he shrugged it off, and he felt the dig of her fingers in his back then the flat of her palms exploring him.

It was their second kiss, yet their mouths were adoring each other's and they were locked in the same urgent tune. He could feel the passion beneath and he pressed in hard. They were a tangle of legs and hot, dirty kisses, and what she lacked in experience was made up for by the instinct that pressed them on.

She felt his hand on her legs, pushing the skirt of her dress up, and she didn't care—in fact, she wanted the same.

Then that same hand moved between them, slipping between their melded bodies, and he lifted his hips and unbuckled his belt.

'Abe…'

That word reminded him she was a virgin for, God knew, his body had forgotten. And then he felt her hand there, at first to halt him, but then she just felt him for a moment, hot and hard beneath her palm.

'Oh…' Her word came out in a shudder and she held him some more, feeling the velvety smooth skin and the strength beneath.

She was on the edge of somewhere she had never been, so Abe got back to kissing her, deep, urgent kisses, so that she did not lose her pace.

And he wasn't taking her, she was half-dressed and panties on, but he was pressing into her and she was lifting into him.

He'd never so urgently pursued another's pleasure, but he demanded it now.

Abe took her hands and held them over her head and he kissed her hard and felt her resisting almost the pleasure she was on the very edge of. And she rued being a virgin for a second, only because had she not been, she knew he would have taken her then.

Abe would have taken her hard and fast on the sofa and she would have let him, and with that thought, with Abe pressing into her, she shattered. He felt her tense and the heat of her face on his cheek and the exquisite moan, and he held on for dear life not to join her, just kissing her red face and smoothing her damp hair, now plastered to her cheeks, and telling himself the wait would be worth it.

'Come on,' he told her, and she heard his voice

breathless, and he stood, tucking himself in. 'Come to my—'

'Abe...'

She was a little stunned as she sat up to find that the lights were on, for locked with him it had felt as if the world had gone the most decadent shade of black.

It was supposed to have been a kiss, except she'd been lost in the moment and drunk in the heat that they'd made together. It surprised her how normal the room looked. The glasses on the table were upright, the lights were on, and everything was in place, except a thoroughly rumpled Naomi, who he now wanted in his bed.

Except she wasn't ready for that and in truth wasn't sure that she'd ever be.

Naomi came with a heart attached.

She pulled her dress up over her breasts, just a little embarrassed to be half-naked now.

His shirt was on the floor, and though his trousers were done up again, she could see how aroused he was; more, she could feel that energy still in the room. She wanted to take his hand, she wanted to be led to his bed, but she did not want the pain that would surely follow in the days or weeks to come.

'I can't, Abe,' Naomi said. 'I can't just be a distraction.'

'Where did that come from?'

'Because I am one,' Naomi hotly responded. Abe was hurting tonight, she knew. He was raw about his father and breaking up with Candice and she was a safe bet because in a few weeks she'd be gone.

And when she had, Abe Devereux would be someone she'd hear about in passing through her friend, or maybe see on the rare occasion that she was here.

And he'd forget her, of course he would.

Whereas she'd be left with a broken heart.

'Abe, I've never been a relationship. Until you I hadn't kissed anyone, let alone slept with anyone.'

Clearly it didn't daunt him. 'Isn't it time to change that?'

Ah, but though she might be innocent Naomi wasn't a fool so she pressed him a little. 'I doubt we're talking relationships.'

He gave a half-laugh. 'Naomi, I'm terrible at them.'

'So you mean sex?'

It sounded clinical and it might even have felt it, except he didn't answer from a distance. Instead, he came and sat down beside her and did the nicest thing. He helped as she wrangled her arms back into her dress.

'How about,' Abe said, and for her he raised his game, 'when you're done here, I take you away?'

'Away?'

'To Cabo.'

She frowned, never having heard of it.

'Cabo San Lucas,' he said, and he told her about his Mexican hideaway and private stretch of white beach, and it was everything, he decided, that she deserved. 'The weather will be beautiful,' he told her, 'the sea like glass…' He was persuading her yet warming to the idea himself, and so used was he to getting his own way with women that it took a moment to realise she was shaking her head.

'And we'll sleep together?' Naomi checked.

'No,' he said immediately, his voice dripping with sarcasm. 'We'll have separate rooms and play charades at night. Of *course* we'll sleep together.'

There was a part of her that wanted to shoot her hand up, and shout, *Me, please*, but there was a deep scar that ran through her heart, a birth trauma almost, except it hadn't faded with time.

And it ached its warning now.

It throbbed in her chest and it reminded her of the hurt she'd endured and warned her there could be so much more to come.

'Then the answer's no.'

He didn't get it, he just didn't. 'I've told you, I'm no good at relationships.'

'Then you're no good for me.'

It was the hardest thing she had ever said. *The* hardest thing, but sex to Abe was as easy as flicking on the light on the way in.

She, on the other hand, would be left carrying that light—a torch named Abe.

And, no, Abe didn't get it. One minute she'd been hot in his arms, the next he was practically offering her a honeymoon vacation, yet still she'd pulled back. 'You'll be telling me soon that you're saving yourself for marriage.'

She'd never really thought of it like that, but that was what Abe did—he made her explore who she was. 'I suppose I am.'

He looked suitably aghast.

'I don't know if it will ever happen for me, Abe, but, yes, I guess I am waiting for that. The simple fact is that I can't just loan out my heart in return for a fortnight in Cabo San… Cabo San Wherever.'

Even if she'd love to.

Even if every inch of her body felt as if it were screaming in silent protest as her decision was made. 'I don't expect you to understand.'

He didn't.

Because the worst part of no was that both their bodies screamed yes.

There was the scent of sex in the air and her nipples were thick beneath her dress and her eyes were still glassy from her climax.

His weren't!

'I'm sorry if I…' she attempted as she saw him to the door.

'Stop apologising,' he snapped.

'Very well.'

''Night, Naomi,' Abe said for the second time in her quarters, but he wouldn't be leaving with his tail between his legs.

This time he kissed her goodnight.

It would seem that that was allowed in her virgin world.

A deep, hot, passionate kiss and he prised her mouth open with his tongue, and when her hands shot to his head as she kissed him back, he removed one and moved it, unresisting, down and held it over his thick length.

Now he pulled his mouth away.

And, yes, he left her wanting.

As was his intention.

And by the time he'd made it to his bedroom for the first time Abe did have a wish list—Naomi Hamilton in his bed by Christmas.

Pleading!

CHAPTER EIGHT

Bergamot, wood sage, juniper *and* vanilla.

His delectable scent was in the hall and still on the stairs as she made her way downstairs the next morning.

Naomi had deliberately come down late in the hope of avoiding him.

It would seem that she hadn't.

Naomi felt like a sniffer dog picking up scent as she headed to the kitchen. She wanted to scuttle back up the stairs but pressed on, determined to keep to her usual routine and not appear to be avoiding him, but when she got there, unusually, *thankfully*, Naomi found that the door was closed.

She could hear Abe's low voice coming from behind it, and she quickly realised it was closed for a reason.

Abe must be speaking to Barb about Jobe.

She headed back upstairs, made coffee in her little kitchen and found a muesli bar lurking at the bottom of her bag, and decided that would just have to do.

It didn't.

And she couldn't hide in this room, avoiding him.

Merida wasn't due back for ages and would hardly demand that she be here, waiting for her, so Naomi decided to head out.

She walked over to the park and once there she replayed last night over and over in her mind.

It had been breath-taking.

Literally.

Even now, she stopped walking, simply recalling last night.

Naomi had always just pushed down that side of her. She had shied away from boys and later men, yet she was herself with Abe. Despite his fierce reputation, despite his bad name. Not once, for even a second, did she feel anything other than safe around him.

Safe enough to be herself around him. To discover herself even.

She was quite sure she should be feeling embarrassed and awkward, but she wasn't. She felt sad, about the conversation taking place in the house, and sad for herself that she had gone and fallen for a man who would give her more than she had ever had, and who would leave her with nothing.

Abe didn't even offer hope.

Had he said they could try, maybe see if they worked, then Naomi doubted even wild horses could drag her from his bed,

So rather than keep looking back at the house, she walked on. Better that than run back to the house and tell him she'd changed her mind and, yes, please, take her to San…wherever it was and make love to her over and over.

She walked for a good hour, till she stood in the very place where they had first kissed, and she wished, how she wished, that she'd had the courage to say yes to him. Wished she could have had the courage to throw caution to the wind and just said yes to one wild, crazy night.

But she hadn't.

So rather than wishing for the impossible, and one night in his arms, she went and bought a hot dog instead.

For once, it didn't help.

'There you are.' Barb smiled when Naomi returned. 'I was just saying to Merida I thought you might be doing the harbour cruise.'

'No, I just went for a walk,' Naomi said, and looked at Barb's face for signs she'd been crying, or any sign really that *the conversation* had taken place, but she looked, well, just like Barb. 'Is everything okay?'

'Everything's fine,' Barb said. 'We had such a lovely night.'

Naomi headed up the stairs and met Merida coming down them.

'Where's Ava?' Naomi asked.

'Asleep.' She was carrying a bag from the hotel, which she handed to Naomi once they were in her little living room.

'What's this?'

'A robe from the hotel's gift shop.'

It was gorgeous, the fabric was very thick and soft, and it was so heavy that for a second Naomi's mind flitted to her luggage, but then she reminded herself that she didn't have to think like that now.

She might need excess luggage this time, but she would soon have a home. Things might not have worked out between herself and Abe, but she hoped that she would get to tell him just how much he had helped her last night.

'How was *Night Forest*?' Merida asked, oh, so casually.

'Wonderful!'

'And Sabine?'

'Terrible,' Naomi said dutifully, and they both laughed. 'No, she was amazing, but I just know that you would have been too. How was Ava?'

'She was cranky,' Merida admitted. 'But we got there. Khalid came up to the suite for a drink before dinner and met her, and she was perfectly behaved then.'

'Was it tense?'

'Not at all! Can you believe that Abe backed down?'

'Really?'

Merida nodded. 'He didn't even come to dinner. He told Ethan that right now he's got more to worry about than placating a sheikh...' She let out a hoot of laughter. 'I gather that Candice finally saw sense and dumped him. Good for her.'

Naomi wondered what Merida's reaction would be if walls could speak!

'So it's all sorted?' Naomi checked. 'The Middle East stuff?'

Merida nodded. 'It seems to be. Khalid's even staying on for the Devereux ball. Mind you, as nice as it was to have a night away, it made me realise I don't want to go. I am not black-tie-ball ready. Either physical or mentally. It's really catty, apparently, and anyway it's your birthday. I'm not leaving you on your own. We can have cocktails and watch the red carpet on live-stream—'

'Merida,' Naomi interrupted, 'you know I don't like a fuss on my birthday. Don't make excuses, it's fine not to want to leave Ava. She'll only be three weeks old.'

'That's just it. And it's not just the night, it's getting ready and all that it entails. I just want to stay home with my baby. I hope that Jobe understands.'

So too did Abe.

He left the office at lunchtime and a short while later walked into his father's hospital suite and saw him resting back on his pillows and looking out of the window to the reservoir. Abe wondered what his father was thinking and he just stood there for a moment, taking it in—the precious time left where he still had a father he could turn to.

If only he would allow himself.

'Jobe…' Abe watched as his father snapped out of his trance and then turned and gave him a tired smile. 'Do you think you might be able to stick around for a while longer?'

Jobe gave a tired laugh. 'Why's that, then?'

'Because I need your advice.'

'Well, they say if you live long enough you see everything once…' Jobe responded. 'What is it you want?'

Abe could tell that Jobe didn't really believe that he needed his father's take on whatever was on his mind, but Abe wasn't placating his father. 'I really could use some guidance. I think you're right and that I should take Naomi to the ball—she deserves an amazing night.'

'Then what's stopping you?'

'I'm not at all sure that she'll agree to go.' He didn't say why. 'But even if she did I'm rather certain that Ethan and Merida would talk her out of it. They'll need her to babysit.' There was an edge to his voice at the final part, and inside Jobe smiled.

'Well, Ethan was just in and said that Merida's not up to a black-tie ball.' He gave his son a wink. 'I'll tell them it's my idea, they're not going to argue with me.' He patted his son's hand. 'I'm sure we can come up with a plan.'

They did, and it took a few days to thrash it all out, deciding it best not to tell Ethan and Merida until the eve of the ball.

And certainly not to let on to Naomi.

Naomi, with time to think about it, would work out a million reasons why she couldn't go.

It had to be a surprise.

'Just avoid her,' Jobe said, 'until the day of the ball.'

Abe tried.

There were places to be and people to see, and what's more there was suddenly more life in Jobe. From having little to do with the details of the ball this year so far, suddenly he wanted everything run past him.

It was a very busy few days.

And not all of them pleasant.

Candice had not taken the break-up well and there were a lot of meetings between Abe and his attorney.

He stood in his office looking out at a cold grey winters day and refused to be screwed over. 'We weren't married,' Abe pointed out. 'It was a contracted agreement.'

'And one that you're breaking.'

'That's covered,' Abe pointed out. 'There are get-out clauses…' And then he stopped, because that's what he did of late.

Since Naomi had come into his life, more and more he was trying to do the right thing—with Khalid, with his father, but, goodness, Candice took every bit of goodwill and milked it for gold.

'She can have the apartment for a further six months.'

Candice wanted twelve.

Abe stormed out of his office, slamming the door behind him, and was pulling on his coat, ready to head down in the elevator and cool off, when he saw her.

Or rather them.

There was Merida, Ava in her pram, and their very awkward-looking nanny.

'Hi, Abe.' Merida gave him a tight smile. 'We just came in to show off Ava…'

He just stalked past them, and Naomi closed her eyes and asked herself how, *how*, she could be so crazy about the kind of man who didn't even stop and say hi to his niece.

But then he halted and looked into the pram and said, of all things, 'Good morning,' to a three-week-old, and then he gave a curt nod to Merida.

And he offered *nothing* to her.

It had almost killed her that since that night she hadn't seen him and now that she had, Naomi hurt even more.

And that hurt was compounded on the eve of her birthday.

There was a rather mad rush on as Jobe had asked that Ethan bring Merida and Ava to see him that night. 'He wants us all to watch the montage we've put together for the ball. Abe too,' Ethan explained to Merida as Naomi dressed Ava.

'Abe will see it tomorrow.'

'I guess…' Ethan agreed, changing his tie. 'I guess he just wants us to see it together.'

'Has Jobe seen it?' Merida asked.

'Not yet.'

They chatted away, as couples did, and then, halfway up the poppers on Ava's little cherry-red suit, came the conversation Naomi had been dreading.

'Who's Abe taking?'

'His latest.'

Naomi messed up the poppers and had to undo the top half and start again.

'Who?'

'I can't keep up with the names.'

It was just a throw-away comment. Such a little thing so that neither noticed Naomi's pale face as she handed Ava over.

'I don't know how long we'll be,' Merida said as she gave Naomi a quick kiss. 'It depends on Jobe.'

'Don't rush back for me,' Naomi said. 'I think I might just head off to bed.'

Which she did.

Naomi peeled off her jeans and top and sat on the

bed in her knickers and bra and did her damnedest not to cry.

Abe had moved on.

She'd expected no less.

Of course he would take someone else to the ball.

'No way,' Jobe said.

He was holding Ava as he watched the montage that had been painstakingly put together. Merida was sitting in the chair beside them as his sons stood, awaiting his verdict. 'It looks like I'm already dead. Use that one next year and put up some clips of me dancing.'

'The ball's tomorrow,' Ethan pointed out.

'Then you'd better crack on,' Jobe retorted. 'But first…'

He *told* them what would be happening.

'No way.' It was Ethan's turn to say it. He gave a curt shake of his head as Merida cast him an urgent glance.

Abe had expected nothing less from his brother, who, now married, had made himself the moral majority.

'Absolutely not.' Ethan looked straight at Abe. 'You can't have him take Naomi to the ball.'

Oh, there wasn't an argument bedside, but the Devereuxes were not the type to let a little thing like death get in the way of a heated discussion.

'But why not?' Jobe frowned. 'You two aren't

going and Abe has to take someone and Naomi's a lovely young lady. As well as that, tomorrow's her birthday. Why shouldn't she be treated to a glitzy night out?'

'It's the company she'll be keeping that concerns me,' Ethan said, and again shook his head. 'No.'

'So you're the type of boss,' Abe checked, 'who dictates what his staff does on their night off. Assuming she gets a night off on her birthday.'

That derisive note was back to Abe's voice. He did *not* like the fact that Naomi was employed by his brother. And it wasn't just snobbery, more he could not stand that he had to go to his younger brother to even take Naomi out. However, he acknowledged that for tomorrow to work, he did indeed need their help.

'Of course I don't dictate what she does in her free time,' Ethan snapped. 'I just wouldn't encourage her to be spending it with you.'

'Well, I think a night out on the town is just what she needs.' Jobe smiled. 'There are a few of the nurses from here going. I'll tell them to look out for her if Abe gets waylaid. I want this, boys…' he told them.

'Boys?' Ethan checked.

'How about,' Abe suggested, 'we leave it for Naomi to decide?'

'Jobe.' Merida found her voice then. She'd been so taken aback at the thought of her shy friend on

Abe's arm at the rather daunting ball that she'd been stunned into silence. 'While it's a lovely idea, women spend months preparing for this night. Dress fittings, spa trips, you can't just spring something like this in on her the day before the event.'

'I agree,' Jobe said. 'I think it better that you tell her tomorrow.'

CHAPTER NINE

'HAPPY BIRTHDAY TO YOU...'

Barb, as she did for all staff on their birthdays, carried a huge tray into the bedroom as she sang a tuneless rendition of 'Happy Birthday'.

'Breakfast in bed!' Naomi sat up. She had completely forgotten about the promise of breakfast. 'How lovely.'

'Not just any breakfast,' Barb said. 'All my best dishes are there.'

There were scrambled eggs with lox, but when Naomi took a taste of the briny smoked salmon she reached for water. And there was *bialys*, round bread with the dent filled in with caramelised onions, and a serving, too, of breakfast potatoes, and it was all topped with bacon crisped to near extinction.

'Take your time,' Barb said.

For someone who loved their food, it was the best, and as she ate, Naomi stuffed down the hurt and planned her day off, *determined* to make the most of it.

She would go on the river cruise, Naomi decided, and then she'd do some last-minute shopping.

And that took care of today, but she could not bear to think of tonight.

Merida's suggestion that they have cocktails together and watch the live-stream of guests arriving sounded like a form of slow torture to Naomi.

She'd have to wriggle out of it, Naomi decided as she dressed, though she had no idea how.

As Naomi came down the stairs with her tray, Bernard was kneeling beneath the Christmas tree, adding presents to the pile, and he smiled when he saw her.

'Happy birthday, Naomi.'

'Thank you.'

'Once you've dropped that in the kitchen, can you go and give Merida a hand with Ava? They're putting up stockings in the drawing room.'

'Sure,' Naomi said. 'I didn't hear them up…'

She pushed open the drawing-room door and there were Ethan, Merida, Ava and Barb all standing by a table, and on it there was gorgeous birthday cake and for the second time that morning she was greeted with song.

'You know I don't like a fuss,' Naomi pleaded.

'This year you're getting one,' Merida said.

Barb had bought her a huge scarf and from Ava there were long silver earrings.

'She has very good taste.' Naomi smiled, privately

wondering where on earth she'd ever wear them—a baby's little fingers tangled up in one would have her earlobe off.

'This is from Ethan and me,' Merida said, and handed her a pale gold envelope. The paper was thick and heavy and as she took out the card inside Naomi frowned as she read it.

'A spa day?' She couldn't keep the question from her voice, and for a moment she wondered if Merida had gone completely mad. Naomi was the last person to go to a spa day, especially one in New York.

God, the women would all be hovering around the hundred-pound mark!

'Thank you,' Naomi duly said. 'I'll look forward to that.'

'You don't have to wait.' Merida smiled. 'It's for today.'

'Today?'

'Yes. You are not to do anything other than be thoroughly pampered…'

'Merida, no…' Oh, she hated saying it, but thanks to Abe she was becoming quite proficient in its use. 'It's a lovely idea and everything, but it's Christmas tomorrow, I've got far too many things that I need to do today.'

'You *have* to go to the spa today because tonight,' Merida said, and then went a little pink, 'you're going to the Devereux ball.'

'No.' Naomi immediately shook her head. 'I can't.'

'You can. It's Jobe's gift to you.'

Naomi felt sick.

Oh, it might not sound a big deal to some, but Naomi so rarely went out.

And certainly not to black-tie balls.

And while it was the most wonderful thought and a gorgeous invitation, she simply could not face it. 'Merida, I shan't know anyone.'

'Jobe's thought of that.' Ethan spoke then, and she caught a tiny look that flashed between him and Merida. 'Abe's going to take you.'

She would wake up soon, Naomi decided, because it was like being stuck in a nightmare.

Yes, any minute now Barb would come singing through her door.

Except everyone stood smiling at her.

She thought of Abe's gritted jaw when Jobe had suggested it, and his utter dismissal of her when they had stopped by the office.

Then she thought of his embarrassment at having her on his arm on this most prominent night.

Oh, he fancied her, she knew that.

But it was a between-the-sheets thing, Naomi was sure.

And while he might be prepared to have sex with her on a private beach, he would not, Naomi was positive, want her by his side at such a high-profile event.

'Merida, please put your magic wand away. I don't

want to be foisted on Abe and I do not want to go to the ball.'

'Naomi…' Merida saw her friend was struggling but she just made it worse. 'Abe will be working the room all night. Khalid will be there and, I promise, Ethan has asked him to look out for you. He's an utter gentleman. And Jobe has two of his favourite nurses going with their husbands…'

'What about Abe, what does he have to say about this?'

'He wants what his father wants,' Merida said.

And she must remember those words, Naomi thought to herself.

He'd been dragged into it by Jobe, possibly not screaming as she doubted Abe had the emotional capacity towards her for that, but still he was doing this to please Jobe. But that meant tonight Abe would be punching above his weight, and not in the usual sense.

Naomi was not being self-effacing but she was not his usual type and she knew it.

It was Merida who calmed her down.

She waved Ethan and everybody off and then sat on the couch with Naomi, who was still clutching the card from the spa. 'Abe will be working the room. You'll hardly have to see him. Just one duty dance and then you can drink Manhattans all night long.'

She'd wished for this, Naomi realised.

Standing in Central Park, she'd wished for one more night in his arms.

And she felt a jumble of things.

Nervous.

Reluctant.

Yet also incredibly, terribly excited.

This was a real black-tie ball and it was the only time she would ever get to attend one.

And she'd dance with Abe.

Even one duty dance from him she would take.

Naomi knew, absolutely, that she must not get ahead of herself. It wasn't a date. This family did this sort of thing all of time and clearly Jobe had been angling for it.

She felt sick.

A little dizzy.

But she was starting to get excited now.

'Bernard's going to take you to the spa now, and don't be shy when you're there,' Merida warned.

'No.'

'Naomi, I mean it. I had a hell of a time when I first got here. I had this stylist, Howard, and he talked down to me all the time. Don't let them.' She held her friend's hands. 'Be yourself and just enjoy it.'

'I have to get some presents…'

'I can get something for you for Barb. Who else?'

'Jobe.'

'I'll think of something. Anyone else?'

Naomi shook her head. She certainly wasn't going to let on to Merida that she'd wanted to get something for Abe.

It was too late for that now.

Naomi would not be intimated at the spa.

Hell, that part came later when she stood with Abe alongside Manhattan's finest.

And so she walked into the spa with her head held high.

Blushing, but her head high.

'Ah, yes.' The receptionist didn't really smile when Naomi gave her name. 'Jobe asked that we squeeze you in. Come this way.'

It was impossible to relax as she sat down in the chair and was eyed up by the colourist and the skin technician.

Together they looked at her hair, her nails, her bone structure. The only thing they didn't do was pull back her gums and check her teeth.

'So, you're one of the nurses?' the skin technician said, and made her a charity case straight away. 'Jobe is so-o-o generous.'

'Actually, no, I'm…' Naomi chose not admit to being the nanny. 'I'm a friend of the family.'

Ms Skin Technician did not raise her eyebrows, Naomi wasn't sure she'd be able to, but her glance to her colleague said it all.

'And do you have a date tonight?' the colourist asked.

'I do,' Naomi said. 'Abe.' There was a not-so-tiny pause and Naomi found out she wasn't such a nice person after all as she suppressed a self-satisfied smile, and just for a moment she lived the dream.

'Abe Devereux?' they both simultaneously checked.

'Yes.' Naomi nodded. 'Abe's taking me to the ball tonight.'

Now they got out their wands because, at the dropping of his name Naomi went from squeezed-in charity case to seriously spoiled.

First oil was placed in her hair and she was sent to relax in a small pool with an eye mask on.

Then another pool.

And then she was massaged from head to toe with rough salt and after their that she was rinsed off and then pummelled and plucked and trimmed in places even Abe, despite their tryst on the couch, had never seen.

It was, though, the best gift she'd ever been given and despite feeling so shy at first, it turned out to be an amazing day.

As she lay having her shoulders rubbed, there was an oil they used that was so utterly fresh and relaxing she asked if she could buy some.

There was actually a very exclusive gift shop and, wrapped in a dark robe, waiting to be made up, Naomi browsed, deciding to purchase a bottle of the oil and a vaporiser.

For Jobe.

For Barb she got the biggest bottle of bath oil and some scented candles and at the last minute she added a pretty tin of extraordinarily expensive mints to her pile.

'They'll fit nicely in my purse,' Naomi said to the sales assistant.

But, yes, it was in case he kissed her.

'Tell us about your dress,' she was asked as she moved to the final chair.

'It's black,' Naomi said, because it was the only one she had.

'By whom?'

And she would not admit to having bought it online so she fudged instead and gave the name of a designer she knew Merida had worn.

'What look are you aiming for tonight, Naomi?'

And she looked in the mirror and didn't know how to answer that for a moment.

She didn't know how to be beautiful and she didn't think she could ever look as if she belonged.

'Do you want to leave it to us?' the senior clinician checked. 'We're very good.'

They were.

Naomi had never known her hair could be so smooth and glossy and it was gently pinned up, so that some curls fell at the front.

It was a look she had tried several times herself and failed to achieve.

Then the make-up artist set to work.

Her skin was incredibly pale, and they left it at that, just smoothed her complexion out. Her make-up was, in fact, very subtle, with neutral colours and soft lips, the only exception to that being her eyes. Though initially delicately shaded, the look was finished off with lashings of eyeliner, and when Naomi declined false lashes, they went to town with the mascara.

It was odd looking back at her reflection, but there was no big reveal because time was running out.

Instead, she put on a robe and was bundled into the car, like a child in pyjamas being taken home from her parents' night out.

Only Naomi's night was just starting.

Merida was waiting for her and it would seem the countdown had started because she practically raced her up the stairs.

'Happy birthday,' Merida said, once they were in Naomi's rooms and she handed her another parcel.

'You already got me a present.'

'Well, I got you another one,' Merida said.

They were silver knickers and the most amazing lacy silver bra.

'Abe is not to see them,' Merida warned, and Naomi laughed. 'I mean it, Naomi. You look stunning, even in a robe. And I know he's devastatingly handsome, but trust me when I say he's wrong for you.'

'I've already worked that out, Merida.'

'No, I know I've told you but you have to listen to me—'

'Merida,' Naomi interrupted. 'Leave it, please.'

'Naomi?'

And Naomi had seen it more times than most—the utter fog a new mother descended into, and the frown that formed when they first came blinking out of it and found that the world as they had once known it had completely changed.

'What am I missing here?' Merida asked.

'Not much,' Naomi said, and she tried not to cry on her new eyelashes as she held her friend's hands. 'But I know his reputation, and I also know why women fall so easily for him. He can be wonderful. So wonderful that you could choose not to believe the warnings and very easily believe you were the only girl in the world. I *know* all that.'

'Oh, Naomi. I'd never have agreed to this if I'd known. I—'

'No,' Naomi interrupted. She'd had the whole day to think about it. 'I'm so happy we get tonight and for a minute I can dance with him, and...' Well, she didn't go into detail but she wanted this night. Even if Abe had been put up to it by his father, even if she was a bit of a charity case, Naomi wanted a night on and in his arms. 'I want to go the ball.'

'Then you shall.' Merida smiled and held open the bedroom door. 'And I don't get fairy godmother status for this. It was Abe...'

On her bed was the very dress she had tried on that day while he'd been fitted for his suits, and Naomi offered silent thanks to Felicia, who must have remembered her size.

'Oh, my…'

She had never owned anything so heavenly before and then she checked herself. 'Is it on loan?'

'No,' Merida said. 'It's yours.'

And where would she keep it? Naomi thought as she held up the decadent garment. The top was boned so it would fill up half a case, but she'd pay excess luggage for the rest of her life rather than ever let it go.

Merida left Naomi to get dressed but, once alone, Naomi stood staring at the gorgeous dress. Beside it were shoes and a bag. Every detail had been taken care of and she had never felt so looked after before.

The deep violet of the dress and the stunning make-up brought out the blue of her eyes and her porcelain skin, and her new silver earrings gleamed at her throat.

'My bust looks huge,' Naomi said, and if there was one detail she could change, she wished the dress had straps because she felt as if her breasts might fall out.

'It looks amazing,' Merida assured her. 'You look amazing.'

'I need a wrap…'

'I've got a black one that will go beautifully,' Merida said. 'Oh, Naomi, you look completely stunning.'

'Honestly?'

'Absolutely. Abe's not going to know what's hit him.'

On the contrary.

Abe had always known she was a beauty and when she came to the top of the stairs and he saw her, it was simply confirmed.

From her hair to the paleness of her arms and the spill of creamy cleavage, he drank in the view.

She lifted the skirt of her dress and on unfamiliar heels walked down and then paused. Not from nerves, more that she too could take in his absolute splendour.

The wanted-poster look might be gone—his black glossy hair had been cut to perfection and he was cutthroat-razor shaved—but she had never wanted someone more in her life.

His suit was divine, and he stood tall and elegant and utterly still except for the glint of desire in his eyes.

And when it was just them, when he looked at her like that, all self-doubt ceased.

That he wanted her, still.

That he always had, made her feel beautiful.

And when she came to the foot of the stairs and inhaled his cologne, Naomi had to dig her newly neutral, manicured nails into her palms so as not to lift her hand to feel his smooth jaw.

And then she looked down and over his left arm

was draped violet velvet. Abe had taken care of every detail tonight. 'Happy birthday,' he said, and wrapped her in the cape she had not dared to try on that day.

The lining was silk and she felt its coolness as he draped it around her and then the weight of the velvet.

Naomi found out then how it truly felt be taken care of.

With this single moment he made up tenfold for the million lonely moments she had known in her life.

And even as she warned herself not to go there, it was way too late.

Naomi knew then that she was in love.

'Ready?' Abe checked.

And she hesitated, because the private realisation of the depth of her feelings was confronting, but there was no real time to examine it. Merida was dashing down the stairs with the wrap she no longer needed and Ethan had come out from the drawing room to see them off.

'Bernard's waiting…' Ethan told them.

'I can't wait to hear how it all went.' Merida smiled. 'If Ava's up when you get in…'

And her words incensed Abe.

How dared they wait up.

They were carrying on as if she were a lamb being led off to slaughter, and having seen Naomi into the waiting car he marched back up the steps to where his brother and sister-in-law stood.

'Do you insist that your staff be back at a certain time?' Abe demanded.

'Of course not,' Merida gritted. 'But Naomi's a friend.'

'And yet you give her one night off in seven and then dictate how she spends it.'

Yes, he was still a bastard.

'Abe,' Ethan warned. 'Don't take it out on Merida. With your reputation, she has every right to be concerned.'

'And yours is so lily white?' Abe checked, and he looked at them both. Hell, he loved them but he would be dictated to by no one, especially in this. 'Butt out!'

He turned and walked briskly down the steps and he could see Naomi's anxious face peering out of the car, making sure that everything, everyone was all right.

And she just stopped him in his tracks, for how could he be angry at two people who were looking out for Naomi?

Abe knew his own reputation after all.

He turned on the steps and, swallowing his pride, he walked back up them.

'You have nothing to worry about,' he told them. 'I'll take perfect care of her.'

Abe fully intended to.

CHAPTER TEN

IT SHOULD HAVE been a gorgeous drive to the hotel.

The snow was falling lightly over a snow-capped Central Park and had he held her hand it would have been utterly perfect, except he silent drummed his fingers on a long, suited thigh.

'Do you have to greet everyone?' Naomi asked.

'God, I hope not,' Abe said. 'Don't worry, there'll just be loads of air-kissing for you. You don't have to remember anyone's name.'

He was trying to put her at ease, but she could feel his tension.

Perhaps, now they were near, he was rueing the fact he'd agreed to take her, Naomi thought, because while he'd been lovely at the house, he was on edge now.

Naomi went into her bag and prised open her tin of mints, more for something to do than because she wanted one.

Except they weren't mints!

It took a second to register they were mint-flavoured condoms.

Oh, God, Naomi thought, stuffing them back in her bag, terribly glad she hadn't offered him one!

And then, as she stepped out of the car, she suddenly thought how she'd, oh, so casually added them to her purchase, explaining how they'd fit in her purse. Maybe it was nerves but she suddenly stifled a laugh and arrived smiling on the red carpet.

It was Abe who was tense.

She felt as if she had stepped into Christmas when they entered the hotel.

There was a huge scarlet Christmas tree centrepiece in the main foyer that looked as if it were made of velvet. But as her cape was removed and she was handed a single red rose, Naomi saw that the tree itself was made entirely of the most exquisite red roses, each bloom perfect.

'It's beautiful.' Naomi would have loved to linger and just take it all in, but there wasn't time to as Abe was quietly informed her that they were to go straight through.

She held onto Abe's arm as lightly as she could, and tried to slow down her heart rate as they entered the ballroom. It was stunning. The chandeliers dripped Icelandic-looking crystals and despite the warm air she felt as if her breath should blow white. It was so breath-taking that for a moment Naomi simply drank it all in and tried to forgot her nerves.

But as guests arrived, heads turned in her direction.

Naomi tried to tell herself that they were all looking at Abe. After all, a lot of the women here tonight had eyes only for him, yet she could not fail to see the slight surprised reactions at his choice of date for the night.

When she had been introduced to, shaken hands with and been air-kissed by more people than she could possibly remember, Abe told her he had to go and speak to someone. 'I'll leave you in Khalid's safe hands.'

Oh, please, don't, Naomi thought, because she didn't know if her nerves could take it—Khalid was a sheikh prince.

Except he was completely charming.

Dressed in a long gold robe, he looked both exotic and formidable, yet he was delightful.

'It is a pleasure to meet you, Naomi.' His smile was warm and unexpected. 'I have heard a lot about you.'

'I'm a good friend of Merida's,' she replied, assuming that Merida, or perhaps Ethan, must have mentioned her when they were talking about Ava.

'Merida?' he checked. 'Of course. Abe did say you were from England. Ah, so that is how you and Abe met.'

Naomi nodded.

'I have to thank you,' he added.

'Me?'

'For pouring oil on trouble waters. I never thought Abe would agree, but—here we are.'

Naomi assumed he had mixed her up with someone, or that she had lost the thread of the conversation, given how hard it was to concentrate. She could feel eyes on her and sometimes she caught the raised hands as people spoke behind them and asked each other who she was.

The women were absolutely stunning and must have taken rather more than a day to prepare for tonight. They reminded Naomi of tiny hummingbirds, and not just because of their elegant clothes and glittering jewels, but from the dainty sips of their drinks.

Naomi realised she had already drained her glass.

Khalid gestured for another.

'I'd better not,' Naomi said.

'Relax,' Khalid said. 'Enjoy yourself. You look wonderful.'

'I'm not used to wearing…' She didn't want to go into detail, but the bones of her gorgeous dress were digging in just a little and she kept reaching for a strap that wasn't there, and wanting to check her cleavage was behaving, but then Khalid made her laugh.

'I too feel awkward,' he told her. 'Usually in New York I wear a suit, not a robe of gold. But it is a national holiday in my country and so it is appropriate that I represent it.'

Naomi doubted he knew what it was to feel awkward, even for a moment, but it was so nice of him to try and put her at ease that Naomi found she did relax and speak more easily. And it was a blessed relief because she did not want to look as if she needed rescuing. The last thing she wanted was to be a drag on Abe tonight.

She certainly wasn't.

Naomi soon recognised the nurse who had brought Jobe down for the photos with Ava on the day she had arrived in New York, and they chatted.

And then a second before the speeches came a lovely surprise.

'I knew you'd look stunning…'

'Felicia!' Naomi's smile was genuine and wide, thrilled to see another familiar face. 'How lovely to see you.'

'It's even lovelier to see you. I wouldn't be here otherwise.'

Naomi frowned but Felicia explained.

'Abe called and said he wanted to surprise you and could I sort out your dress. I told him about the dress you'd liked and he mentioned how much you'd adored the coat. For my efforts, I got invited to the Devereux ball. Cheers!'

'Thank you so much.' Naomi beamed. 'I can't believe you managed to sort out my clothes and get ready yourself all in a day.'

'A day?' Felicia frowned. 'I've—'

But whatever she was about to say would have to wait because the speeches started at that moment.

And there were many, but they were all very thoughtful and emotional, pointing out Jobe's absence tonight and the equipment the funds from the ball had provided for the children's wing of the hospital where Jobe was a patient.

There was a small montage of footage from the ball over the years, and as she looked at the footage Naomi saw a much younger Jobe, dancing with Elizabeth, his late wife.

And as Naomi looked around some of the women were reaching for handkerchieves and there were murmurs of 'how beautiful' she had been.

And she had been, Naomi thought.

On the outside.

Naomi found her gaze falling on Abe. He stood there, his expression unreadable as he looked at the screen, and she wondered about the thoughts behind his impassive facade.

Yet she knew them a little.

That he had told her some of his past felt like a great privilege. That in this room packed with his acquaintances, colleagues and friends there was a shard of him he had shared with her that so few knew.

Oh, their time together was so precious to her that even if it was fleeting, she treasured each second and would never forget this night when she felt so special and a part of this world.

And then came the final speech, and Naomi found she held her breath as Abe took the microphone.

She wanted to capture in her mind his beauty and the way he held the room, she wanted to embed his features so deeply in her brain that when she closed her eyes in the nights and years to come she would remember even the tiny details.

The darkness of his eyes and his exquisite cheekbones.

And the deepness of his voice.

How he barely smiled as he thanked the room, yet there was no surly note to his tone.

It was just that he rarely smiled.

How he did not waste words as he thanked those present, and he did not repeat all that had been said.

Instead, he shared something new with them all.

'The roses were Jobe's idea. He wanted each woman to have a flower from him tonight. He was aware that some of you will have received roses from him personally over the years…' It was a slight allusion to Jobe's philandering tendencies, but it was said in the kindest way. 'He would like you to accept one more, with his love and thanks.' There was a pause and, Naomi guessed, there might be some women in this room who would be pressing the bloom they held in their hands between pages tonight. She would be, for his was a life to remember, as was this night.

Abe spoke on, and to conclude he said how his father wished he could be there but, though not present, he had insisted that every detail of the night had been run by him.

'I hope,' he said, 'to make him proud.'

And then he looked over at Naomi, and he met her eyes and he smiled.

It was unexpected, and she felt eyes on her as she returned his rare smile, but then forgot about everyone else. Abe had the skill of making you forget there were even others in the room.

So much so that she almost forgot to clap at the end of the speeches.

And when he came over to her and the music started, it was without embarrassment or thought that she took his hand.

Naomi had never been kissed until Abe.

And she had never danced with anyone until tonight.

As he led her onto the dance floor, she didn't care if it was a duty dance if for one dance in her life she was held by him.

But when he held her, when he pulled her into his arms and his hand took hers while the other held her waist, Naomi knew she lied. As she rested her head on his chest, her eyes drifted to the band, and silently pleaded that this dance never end.

He felt the warmth of her skin through the fabric and his palm resisted the urge to drift a fraction lower.

It was Abe who, for the first time, had to focus on his breathing. Who had to stare beyond the fragrant curls and out into the corporate world and remember his vow to himself to be a perfect gentleman tonight.

Then she moved in his arms and her heavy breasts squashed into his chest, and he recalled them naked against his skin on the night she had denied him.

And she felt her heartbeat quicken at the heat from his palm and desire took hold and she closed her eyes in an attempt to resist it.

'Naomi?'

'Yes?'

'I'm going to have to do the rounds soon…'

She nodded and reminded herself that this was work to him. 'That's fine,' she said, and pulled her head back and looked up.

A dangerous mistake.

One only ever read about Abe's scandals.

For all the trysts he'd been caught up in there had never been as much as one single public display of affection.

That ended tonight.

His mouth found hers so easily and both took their fill.

And the band must have read her earlier plea for they played on as the whispers chased each other around the room.

Abe Devereux and *that* woman.

Who no one knew by name.

One thing was certain, though, and both tongues and cameras were clicking tonight.

This kiss may have started on the dance floor but it would end in bed.

Tonight.

CHAPTER ELEVEN

IT WAS NAOMI's night of nights and, quite simply, she wished it would never end.

Even when they left the dance floor as Abe had to go and work the room Naomi felt as if she floated from his arms. She spoke with Felicia, with Khalid and even with strangers, and every now and then he would look over, checking that she was okay.

Naomi felt shielded from the whispers and stares that had plagued her since she had walked in, and in that ballroom indeed she was. There was Abe looking out for her, Khalid and, unbeknown to her, Felicia was too.

The night was starting to wind down and couples were starting to leave, the women still clutching their rose. 'I might nip to the loo,' Naomi said, and Felicia frowned. 'The restroom,' she clarified.

'Good idea.' Felicia nodded. 'I might come with you, there'll be a rush on soon.'

But as they picked their way through the ballroom, Felicia turned to the sound of her name.

'Felicia?'

Naomi also turned at the sound of the voice and saw a very handsome man walking towards them, a curious look on his face. 'It *is* you,' he said.

'Leander...'

Naomi watched as the confident and assertive Felicia, stood, looking stunned, but then she attempted to gather herself. 'Leander, this is Naomi.'

'Naomi,' he said.

Except, as he said it, his eyes never left Felicia's face, and Naomi, who had played a part, perhaps more than most, knew it was time to leave.

No matter.

Naomi wasn't one for moving in a pack and was more than capable of going to the restroom alone.

The possibility that Abe might have asked Felicia to keep a close eye on her never even entered her head.

And with good reason.

Naomi, with her new and fragile confidence emerging, truly had no idea of the snake pit lurking beneath the well-dressed tables or the daggers that were being thrown from behind frozen smiles.

She assumed everyone was as happy tonight as she was.

Naomi washed her hands and as she went into her

purse for her lipstick she saw the little tin that *didn't* contain mints and her final gift was sorted out.

She *would* be with Abe tonight.

And not hesitantly.

A short-lived affair she could live with far more than she could live a life without it.

Naomi did not need San Cabo, or wherever it was, to be with him, or promises he could never keep to be with him.

She heard the band strike up a Christmas song that had always made her cry.

It wouldn't any more, for it would remind him of this night for ever.

In a few moments it would be Christmas, Naomi thought, and she crammed her *mints* back into her purse, ready to head out there for the chance of one last dance, when she heard her name.

'Naomi?'

Naomi turned and smiled at a petite blonde woman in a stunning high-necked red dress.

'You're Naomi, right?'

'Yes?' There was a question in her voice, wondering if she ought to know the woman, or if they'd been introduced for, yes, she looked a little familiar. And then Naomi found out why. She had seen her in photos, of course.

'I'm Candice,' she confirmed.

'Oh.' Naomi really didn't know what else to say

and felt the little colour she had leach from her face and she swallowed nervously.

'Please…' Candice smiled and put out her hand and gave Naomi's arm a reassuring squeeze '…don't feel awkward, I'm very used to all of this.'

Only Naomi *wasn't* reassured and she *did* feel awkward.

'I really ought to get back out there,' Naomi said hurriedly. She knew she was being an utter wimp, but a less than friendly chat with Abe's very recent ex felt uncomfortable, to say the least.

But Candice wasn't letting her go just yet.

'It really is fine.' She gave Naomi another smile, only one that was almost sympathetic. 'I've long accepted Abe's affairs.'

'We're not…' Naomi blew out a breath. She really didn't know what she and Abe were. It was hardly an affair. And at every level Naomi knew too that whatever they had briefly found couldn't last. She knew too that she was just his plus one tonight. But all she wanted was this perfect night and she didn't want Candice getting in the way of that. 'We're not together, as such,' Naomi said, and made to leave.

'Of course you are,' Candice said. 'Abe was just saying to me this afternoon that he was bringing you tonight.'

That stopped Naomi in her tracks and slowly she turned. 'This afternoon?'

'When he came by our apartment.'

Naomi felt sweat trickling between her breasts. 'I thought the two of you...' She halted herself, refusing to be drawn in, but Candice used her small opening wisely.

'You thought we were finished. Is that what he told you?'

Naomi's jaw gritted.

'I guess Abe would say that, but of course we're not finished.'

Naomi found her fire then, just for a second. 'I know that he pays you...'

It was futile, of course.

'Of course he does.' Candice shrugged. 'Abe likes me to look good *all* the time. In fact, I just signed a contract for another year.' She took out her phone and pulled up a document.

'I don't need to see that.'

'Oh, I'd suggest that you take a good look,' Candice said, 'because you really do seem rather clueless as to how this all works. There's reams of it...'

And there was, and even if she tried not to look, she saw the Madison Avenue address and, yes, it was all too sordid for her.

Not that Candice had finished marking her territory and warning Naomi off. 'In a nutshell I just accepted his terms again. I'll turn the other cheek and be back by his side in the new year and back in his bed.'

'Abe said that you don't sleep together.' Naomi

was trying her hardest to keep it together, and she wasn't being a bitch in her response, more trying to explain she would never be involved with Abe if she thought he was with someone.

'And you believed him when he said that?' Candice let out a tinkle of laughter. 'As I said, I accept his affairs, although I have to say…' she looked down at Naomi's full figure '…he's scraping the barrel right now. Maybe he's having a fat phase. Then again, as my friend just said when she saw the two of you dancing, it's always so much harder to get the vehicle serviced when it's snowing.'

As Candice walked off, Naomi felt sick.

She felt embarrassed.

And guilty too.

Because even if nothing much had happened between herself and Abe, deep down Naomi had been hoping that tonight it would.

She admitted it to herself then.

The pampering and preening had all been in the hope of being made love to tonight by him.

Naomi had even accepted that for Abe it could only ever be a fling.

She had lowered her standards over and over to be met by him, all the way down to a one-night stand, but she would never have agreed to tonight had she known that he was still with Candice.

Naomi gripped the sink and tried to hold in the tears, but they had already started to come.

Big fat tears that took with them the lashings of mascara and slid down her cheeks in oily black streaks, and her nose went from white to red with the speed of a supercar's engine.

And that red nose ran too.

She tried to blot the tears with one of the little fluffy hand towels and she tried to hold in the great shuddering sobs, but they were building and women were coming in, and looking at her sideways. And she thought about what Candice's friend had said, about her size and how it was hard to get serviced when it was snowing, and for Naomi it was just all too much.

They were *all* laughing at her, Naomi was sure.

And she was heaping loathing on herself for daring to dream that things could be different, even for one night.

Naomi walked away from the stares in the restroom to the stares in the gorgeous foyer, crowded with people collecting their coats, and it felt as if they turned *en masse* to look at her.

She could not face collecting her gorgeous coat, and she could not imagine going back into the ballroom to find Abe.

There was no point anyway because at the entrance doors to the ballroom she saw the flash of red of Candice's dress. She was talking to Abe and running a hand along the lapel of his jacket and all

Naomi could think in that second was how stunning they looked together.

And she did the only thing instinct told her to, and she fled.

Past the gorgeous people all effortlessly chatting.

And past the doorman, who called her back.

'Do you have a coat, madam...?'

It was like her first day in the city but without all the excitement, without all the hope, because all hope had gone.

She just fled down the stairs and out into the freezing night, losing not just a shoe but her hairstyle too, because her carefully pinned hair all came tumbling down.

And Abe saw her leave.

He had been standing at the doors, shaking hands with a guest while looking out for Naomi, when he'd seen Felicia. 'Where's Naomi?'

'I was just...' Felicia had clearly lost track of her. 'She went to the restroom.'

It was then that he saw Candice making a beeline for him.

She wasn't on the guest list but, of course, he didn't keep the party planners in the loop as to the status of his love life, and this late at night, things must have slacked off. It would seem that Candice had slipped in.

Of course she had. He had been a fool to think she would go quietly.

'Hey.' She smiled and came over.

'What are you doing here, Candice?' he clipped.

'I come every year,' she pointed out. 'Well, I have for the last three. You're looking very smart…' She ran a possessive hand down his jacket and looked right into his eyes.

He should never have attempted to play this nice. The one time he'd tried to the right thing it had backfired spectacularly because as he looked out of the ballroom it was just in time to see Naomi running off.

'What the hell did…?' He didn't even bother asking the rest of the question, he didn't need to hear from Candice what had been said. All he knew was that Naomi was hurting. He pushed past the crowds and the doorman didn't see him coming because he'd gone after Naomi and was retrieving her shoe and trying to call her back, but Naomi had continued to run.

'She's distressed, sir,' he said as Abe approached.

He could see that.

And she was cold.

Freezing, in fact.

And the cars were all a blur as she crossed the road.

'Naomi!' She heard him shouting and she cared not if she was making a scene, she just wanted to get as far away from Abe Devereux as her legs would allow.

Somewhere private where she could cry out loud,

as she hadn't been able to on the day she'd first found out what an utter pig he was.

She made it to the edge of the park before he caught up.

'Leave me alone!" she shouted.

'Come back inside.'

'Never! I'm not going back there. They're all—'

'I've booked us a suite,' he interrupted, but his attempt to soothe only served to incense her.

'Was I such a sure thing?'

Of course she was—Naomi knew that.

He reached for her arm but she shook him off. Naomi was trying to remember if she had money in her bag to get a cab, except with one bare foot and bare arms on a freezing night she was struggling to think. The frigid air delivered more than a cold slap. It was like the pain of stubbing her toe, except it ran the length of her body and did not abate, and she wrapped her arms around herself in a futile attempt to get warm.

'Here...' He held out his jacket but she declined it.

'I want nothing from you.'

'So you're going to freeze to death to prove a point?'

And she very possibly might, because her teeth were chattering and her hair was going stiff, and she was no Cinderella as he pushed her down onto a bench and put his jacket round her shoulders and then pushed her less-than-dainty foot into the shoe.

And he was no Prince Charming because he was telling her off.

'You just can't run off in this weather,' he snapped, making sure her foot was in the shoe 'What the hell were you thinking? If you're going to be with me, you'd better get used to being talked about and not always nicely, and not run off crying every time someone makes a disparaging comment about me.'

'With you,' Naomi sobbed. 'I want to be as far away from you as possible, Abe. Did you sign another contract with her, with Candice?'

'Not now,' he said, and stood, but Naomi wanted answers.

'Were you with her today?'

He didn't respond. In fact, he didn't breathe because the air didn't blow white as he declined to comment.

'I'll take that as a yes,' Naomi answered for him. 'Are you *keeping* her for another year? Agh!' She revolted loudly at the end, for she hated that word, and hated that she'd been reduced to asking him, but that was what this man did—he kept women.

'I was trying to be nice.'

'Nice? You wouldn't know nice…' she attempted, but she couldn't get the rest out. Naomi, who would never hurt anyone, had risen to her feet, and the only reason she didn't pummel his chest was because she knew she might end up sobbing on it.

'Let's not do this here,' Abe suggested.

And she should respond, *Let's not do this at all*, as she had the first time he'd broken her heart, but all she wanted was to get back to the house, pull the covers over her head, and for this horrible birthday to be finished with.

For Christmas to be over and done.

To conclude this.

And so she let him lead her, but she threw off his arm and walked alone.

He called his driver to come over and as they waited, she watched all the beautiful people spilling out of the hotel, and heard shouts of *Merry Christmas* as they climbed into the waiting cars.

It certainly wasn't a merry one for her.

Abe said nothing. He just looked ahead, unable to believe how his meticulously planned night had panned out.

Where are we going?' she asked as they sailed past his father's home.

'To my place,' Abe said. 'I don't particularly want your fan club policing this.'

'My fan club?'

'Merida, Ethan, Barb, Bernard… You've got a lot of people in your corner, you know, my father included.'

And while she was grateful to have them, Naomi looked over at the one she wanted more than anyone in the world.

It was a pointless want.

He might as well be a poster on a teenager's bedroom wall or a film star on the screen he was so unattainable, but for a while there she'd let herself think that she might belong, even for a night, in his world.

His world was stunning, Naomi thought as she stared out of the car window. The streets were wider here and the trees were sparkling with fairy lights. There really was a village feel to the shops, with shutters open, revealing gorgeous displays and Christmas wares. Closed cafés that by day would beckon you in for catch-ups and brunch and she could see why Abe loved it here so much.

'We're here.'

They had turned into a gorgeous tree-lined street and the car pulled up outside a huge brownstone house. She climbed out of the car and, rather than hold his arm, she held onto the rail as she climbed the stoop and then stood as he opened the door to his home.

As she stepped inside, it was luxurious, yes, but it was certainly a home.

The hallway was long, with archways, and there was one staircase leading up and one leading down.

'Come through,' he said, but she did not know where so she followed him down the long hallway, the dark wooden floors softened with a Persian rug that her heels sank into. Beyond the hall she could see a large kitchen and she could almost picture him sitting on one of the stools, sipping coffee. Beyond, Naomi glimpsed a softly lit garden, and it was cruel to be in his home, for now she would picture him here for ever.

Abe pushed open a door and as she stepped through it the delicious scent of pine hit her, and even though it was officially Christmas Day, the sight of a tree gorgeously decorated and beneath it presents added another layer to his lies.

Naomi stood clutching her bag and shivering in his jacket as he lit the fire. He was drenched from melted snow and his hair was as wet as if he'd just come out of the shower.

He'd lit a fire on the night they had met, Naomi recalled. It felt such a long time ago. Then she'd sat, at first innocent to his charms.

She wasn't now.

He'd snaked into her heart that night, Naomi thought.

So much so that when she'd found out about Candice, she'd chosen to believe him when he'd said it was over.

Those dark eyes, that kiss had melted her inhibitions away. She looked at way the shirt clung to his back, recalling her hands sliding over his naked torso as he'd brought her to her first orgasm.

And for him she'd broken all her own rules because she'd been hoping for more tonight.

Instead she stood there dripping wet, and the night ruined, by his fire.

On Christmas morning.

She looked at the ornaments on the mantelpiece, and the tree in the corner with presents beneath and she unearthed another of his lies. 'I thought you didn't bother with Christmas.'

'I don't usually,' Abe said, and with the fire starting he stood. Her absolute lack of faith didn't perturb him, he got why she had none. 'Naomi, how many times do I have to tell you that Candice and I are through?'

'And I'm supposed to believe you? She told me—'

'Why would you listen to her?' Abe demanded.

'Who else would I listen to? You?' Naomi retorted. 'You haven't spoken to me in a week. You couldn't even look at me when I came to your office…'

'I've been cleaning up my life,' Abe said. 'I've been trying to right an awful lot of wrongs. Naomi, I saw Candice this afternoon, yes. And she finally signed a contract that means for another twelve months she can live in the flat, but that's it. I thought I'd sorted it, but I hadn't. I'm sorry for what you went through tonight, but the fact is you're going to have to start trusting me.'

'Trusting you?' The man with the reputation, the man who should come with a warning sign attached, the man she still wanted, even *now*. 'You!' Her purse clattered to floor as she jabbed a finger into his chest. 'I wouldn't trust you if you were the last man…'

Except he was the *first* man.

The first man to really make time for her. The

first man she had wanted and her very first love, and she was terrified that he really was her last, because she couldn't envisage ever feeling this way again.

'Naomi…' He took her angry hand that was jabbing at him and gripped it between their bodies. 'I was going to talk to you when we were alone. I'd booked a suite for after the ball.'

His assumption incensed her. 'You were you so sure that I'd come up?'

'Yes,' he shouted, because he had been sure, and more so on the dance floor, and even more so as she went to pull away the hand he was tightly holding, but she took his with it. He could feel the softness of a heavy breast and the rise and fall of her chest and when her hand released his, Abe's remained. His fingers were like ice on her skin but she did not flinch, and he looked right into her eyes as she looked into his face.

'Well, I wouldn't have come,' Naomi insisted, except her voice was all breathless.

'Liar,' he told her, and then proved that she was with his kiss.

It was rough and demanding but, then, so was she, her tongue duelling with his, and she was pushing him away but only to get to the buttons of his damp shirt.

She barely knew herself.

All the hurt was placed on hold as all her anger morphed into the want she had suppressed for so long. For she would give anything to be bold enough, to dare enough to give in to the desire that screamed in her veins.

'You would have,' he insisted between hot kisses, his hands rough and delicious on her body, roaming her curves and pulling her into to his primed body.

'I would have,' she whimpered, as his mouth located her neck and he kissed her deeply there.

Yes, yes, she would have. She didn't need Cabo San… Oh, why couldn't she remember its name? But, yes, she would have gone up to the suite, Naomi knew, recalling the certainty before Candice had ruined their night. And she thought of what was in her purse, and while she still had a shred of common sense she dropped to her knees to retrieve it.

And down on the floor she heard his voice and for a second froze.

'Oh, Naomi…'

There was this gravelly note to his voice, and his hand came to her hair and it took a moment for her to register he wasn't asking why she was down there.

Did Abe really think…?

She was at eye level with his crotch and simply couldn't *not* touch, and she looked at her unfamiliar, manicured hand, so pale against the black of his trousers as she felt him through the fabric. And Abe made it so easy not to think, to just completely misbehave, because his gorgeous long fingers were making light work of his zip and Naomi felt a little dizzy as he undid his trousers, revealing just how turned on he was.

'I was getting protection,' she attempted, except her voice was all thick and she had to clear her throat before continuing, but before she could he spoke.

'I know you were.'

'You know?'

'I saw them in the car…'

And, of course, a man like Abe wouldn't mistake them for a tin of mints.

'The thought of us has been driving me wild all night,' he told her.

And now didn't seem the time to tell him it had been a complete accident because, right now, she didn't want to be anywhere else. She looked at his thick length, darker than the rest of him yet pale against the black of his suit, and it looked both delicious and crude jutting out, yet she felt her heat tighten with the desire and the ache of needing to see more of him, but Abe had other ideas.

'Taste me,' he said.

She could feel him warm at her cheek and the male scent of him was enticing but she told him her truth. 'I don't know how.'

'Try.'

He sounded breathless. He sounded tense, but not in a way that she'd ever heard, and she pulled back her head and looked up at him.

Oh, this was so not what he'd planned, Abe thought, but in the very nicest of ways.

She must have had too much champagne, Naomi decided, because she kept missing with her mouth, yet she'd only had two glasses.

Then she held him with her hand, and she broached with tentative lips and tasted the tip slowly with her tongue, and his moan was her reward.

His hand came to her cheek and he brushed her hair back and she felt the caresses of his gaze as she kissed down the sides, growing accustomed to the feel of him as he grew to her palm, and then she took him a little way into her mouth.

He tasted soapy and his scent had always driven her wild. His fingers were in her hair, pulling out all the pins that had been so carefully placed there. He was so tall that she was up on her knees, and holding onto his thighs now to steady herself. Abe's hands guided her deeper than she would ever have dared go herself and his ragged breathing brought intense pleasure that had her wanting to sink back on her knees, except she knelt higher and took him deeper. She could feel his restraint, even as he started to thrust.

Naomi could feel her breast spilling out of her gown, and though she'd dreaded it happening all night, it was freeing now.

She felt him swell and his hand push her head down, and it didn't daunt her, it thrilled her, and when he climaxed, the real shock for Naomi was the desire-filled, intimate beats of her own, the pleasure so mutual that it made her feel giddy as she knelt breathless, topless and his.

Always his.

How did he look so immaculate? she wondered as he tucked himself in and, holding out his hand, brought her to stand.

Abe pulled up her dress and tucked her in too, as if he was readying her for church, rather than about to carry her upstairs, but even if she loved him, Naomi did not know this man.

He went and poured two drinks but he drained his in one draught.

'As I said…'

And she frowned as he handed her a drink and then continued the conversation where they'd left it an indecent while ago.

'The press are going to be merciless, and there will be exes selling their stories, but if you're going to be my wife then you're going to have to start trusting me.'

She heard the first bit.

And the last bit.

But there was too much roaring in her ears when she tried to replay the middle.

Did Abe just say she was going to be his wife?

CHAPTER TWELVE

'WIFE?' NAOMI CROAKED.

She really couldn't believe what she was hearing.

Even when he retrieved his jacket, which had long since dropped to the floor.

As he went into a pocket and took out a box, Naomi kept waiting for the punchline, for a mocking flash mob to appear, for this to be some sort of terrible, elaborate joke, for she just did not know love.

'Naomi,' he said. 'That came out wrong...'

He was nervous, Naomi realised as he spoke on.

'I had flowers and champagne and everything planned, but as long as you say yes, I wouldn't change a thing. Will you marry me?'

Naomi stared down at an exquisite marquise-cut diamond set in delicate rose gold and could not quite comprehend it.

'So that I'll sleep with you?'

'In part...' He smiled, but it faded when he looked at a woman who had never known love yet would have been brave enough to risk her heart to him, and he took that very seriously indeed. 'Naomi, when you told me that you wouldn't sleep with me until we were married, I didn't take it that well.' He looked at her. 'I didn't tell Jobe that I was going to ask you to marry me, but I asked for his help to get you to agree to come the ball.'

'Jobe was in on it?'

Abe nodded. 'I needed his help to get Ethan and Merida on side. I knew they wouldn't want me taking you to the ball and, in fairness, I can see why. And I had Khalid looking out for you, and Felicia.' He rolled his eyes. 'She was so good sorting out your dress that I asked her to the ball on the condition she shadow you all night. I know how poisonous that lot can be. A fat lot of good she did.'

Naomi giggled, but then it died in her throat as the magnitude of it all caught up with her. Abe hadn't been ignoring her, instead he had been paving the way for her to be in his life. And then he told her why. 'Naomi. I'm asking you to marry me because I love you.'

And to hear Abe Devereux saying *I love you* felt as if molten gold was being poured into her heart, and she started to believe this was real.

'Do I have to ask you again?' Abe checked, when still she hadn't replied.

'No,' Naomi said, because he did not have to ask

her twice. 'I mean yes, oh, yes, Abe, I would love to marry you.'

'Well, that's all right, then.' He slipped the ring onto her newly manicured fingers and when she looked down she didn't even recognise her own hand, let alone the world he was inviting her into.

And when she looked up into those black eyes Naomi knew it would take for ever to know him, but they had for ever now.

'I love you,' she told him, and, for Naomi, it was the ultimate luxury to share those words with another.

'I know you do.'

'Take me to bed,' Naomi said, and he obliged, taking her by the hand and leading her up the stairs, presumably to paradise.

Except paradise was a lot more like a guest room than the master lair she'd been expecting it to be.

'You've got your own bathroom…' he said.

'Abe?'

'You wanted to wait until we were married,' he pointed out. 'We've come this far…'

'Oh, no! You can't just leave me like this,' Naomi pleaded. She was in love and in lust, turned on and turned inside out by all that had happened tonight.

And a sated Abe was heading off to bed!

'Hell, isn't it?' Abe said as he gave her a light kiss and wished her goodnight.

'Abe, please…' she said, but the door was closed.

His Christmas wish had come true.

Naomi Hamilton in, okay, a guest bed, rather than his own.

But she *was* pleading.

'Happy Christmas.'

Those were the words she woke to on the best Christmas Day yet.

There was snow on the window and there was the sound of carols being sung outside somewhere, and there was a ring on her finger.

No bells on her toes, but she was quite sure, if she asked, Abe would oblige.

Then again? 'Are you still on a sex strike?' Naomi smiled, and stretching luxuriously realised she'd slept in for the first time ever on Christmas morn.

'I am,' he told her. 'You don't have to be, though, I'm more than willing to repeat last night.'

'Two can play at that game,' Naomi said, even if she was blushing to her roots as she said it.

He sat on the bed and he looked at her, all panda-eyed with mascara and smiling as she examined her ring, and at that moment he knew what true happiness was. 'We'd better get married quickly, Miss Hamilton,' he said, squeezing her thigh through the sheet.

'I agree, Mr Devereux.'

She smiled and then he was serious for a tiny moment. 'I meant what I said, if you marry me there will be more to come. If I don't give the press scandal, I don't doubt they'll make it up, or drag in an ex to sell her story. There are going to be a lot of people hoping that this marriage fails…'

'It shan't.'

She said it with such confidence and assertion because she knew it to be true.

The morning, of course, ran away with them. His present to her was a key to the door.

'Your home,' he told her.

And her present to him… Well, Naomi weakened, and suddenly it was edging too close to nine to even think of stopping at his father's for a change of clothes. Abe was all right, of course, but Naomi really had nothing apart from last night's clothes to wear.

'You're going to have to the do the walk of shame,' Abe said.

His driver had Christmas off, so Abe drove them and she looked out at the beautiful streets she was fast coming to love and it dawned on her that this amazing city would be her home.

'I spoke to Barb,' he told her as they drove alongside Central Park on Christmas morning, and Naomi still felt as if she was in a dream. 'I've spoken to all the staff, and they'll all be taken care of. But Barb and Bernard…'

She turned and looked at him.

'They're going to work for me. Us,' he corrected.

'Dad's place is getting too big for her, and I've had renovations done downstairs.'

'The basement?'

'It's stunning. It's got its own entrance and garden—I don't do things by halves…'

No, he didn't.

'But not yet,' he said, 'hopefully not for ages…' Because they all still need Jobe to be here.

'Abe, once I've finished work we can—'

'You're not working for my brother any more.' He glanced over. 'Absolutely not.' And, yes, he was being a snob, but what the hell? 'The only babies you're getting up for from now on are ours.'

'I can't just leave them in the lurch.'

'Oh, please,' he dismissed. 'They can get a proper nanny if they need one, and you can get on with being Ava's aunt.'

'We're here,' he added, before she could argue.

Only how could she possibly argue with that?

He was talking babies already and she had gone from having no one to being a fiancée and soon-to-be aunt…

There wasn't time to dwell on it, though, as they were at the hospital and the press were waiting.

Of course they were, they'd been taking photos on the day his mother had died, so why not now?

Only they weren't just here for Jobe.

They got their shot of Abe Devereux in black

jeans and jumper and the mystery woman in a velvet dress and his jacket from last night.

The same woman he'd been chasing with a shoe he'd retrieved, and who was now wearing a sparkly ring!

'Merry Christmas, Abe,' they called. 'And to the mystery lady…'

Abe made no comment, but then relented. 'Merry Christmas,' he said.

But then the true spirit of Christmas shone, for the cameras went down and their next words were heartfelt. 'Give our very best to Jobe.'

Abe nodded. 'Thanks.'

They walked along the hallway and came to a stony-faced Ethan, who was clearly looking out for them. He was holding tiny Ava, who was wearing a little elf suit and was thankfully sound asleep in her father's arms. 'Where the hell have you two—?' Ethan snarled, and then stopped himself asking the obvious because, still in last night's dress and with slightly tangled hair, it was seemingly clear.

'Go and say hi,' Abe suggested to Naomi, who was thankful to duck into Jobe's room.

'You'll take perfect care of her?' Ethan sneered, as cries of 'Happy Christmas' started up in his father's room. 'The one time I ask you…' And then his voice halted again because there weren't just Christmas greetings being exchanged, there was a cry of delight from Merida, and he heard Jobe actually bark out a cheer.

'Absolutely, I shall be taking perfect care of her,' Abe said to his younger brother. 'Naomi has agreed to become my wife.'

'You and Naomi?' Ethan was sideswiped, sure he'd heard wrongly, but Abe nodded. 'When did this happen—last night?'

'No, it started on the day this little angel was born,' Abe said, stroking Ava's cheek, and then he looked at his brother. 'Would you mind if I borrowed your nanny on New Year's Eve?' Abe checked. Not only was it the hardest night of the year to find a babysitter, there was more bad news to come. 'Oh, and I shan't be returning her.'

It was a *true* family Christmas.

Naomi's first.

And a true family Christmas meant happy bits, amazing bits and more sadness than you dared to show, because grief and its journey was the price of love.

But a life well lived garnered wisdom, and there was plenty still to be shared.

Between the celebrations, congratulations and festivities was a man they all loved, who watched quietly as they chatted about the upcoming nuptials that were now scheduled for New Year's Eve.

Or rather he watched Naomi.

She didn't want a church, and she didn't want anyone other than her and Abe present, even when he suggested they get married here at the hospital.

Ethan would be best man, Ava a flower baby, Merida the matron of honour…

But no.

'We'll get married quietly.' Naomi shook her head as she smiled. 'Just us, and then we can have a drink back here.'

And that suited some. It worked for Ethan but…

'Can I speak to Naomi?' Jobe said. 'Alone.'

'Are you kicking us out?' Abe checked.

He was.

'Why no fuss?' he asked when everyone was gone. 'Is it because of me?'

'I don't need a big wedding.' Tears were pooling in her eyes and she did not want to spoil the happiest day of her life, but he had such wise eyes and they had clicked on that very first day, so she told him the truth. 'Jobe, there's no one to give me away.'

'Could I?' Jobe asked, and he looked at the kindest, sweetest woman who had come into their lives and changed them all. 'Because nothing would make me prouder.'

It wasn't such a tiny wedding.

There were an awful lot of nurses and doctors all helping them to achieve this day and there was Bernard in a suit and Barb in a hat and even a sheikh prince, but today he wore a suit.

And as for the bride, she wore white, because she deserved to.

'It's a myth that people with pale skin can't wear white,' Felicia had told her. She had been forgiven for losing Naomi at the ball.

Just as Abe had moaned about the many shades of black, Naomi had, with Felicia's help, pored over whites and found the perfect one. A snow white that was as pure as the love that had saved them, in the softest silk faille.

The dress hugged her curves and silhouetted her fuller figure, and a Bardot neckline revealed her creamy décolletage to perfection.

She wore her dark hair down and it fell in shiny coils, with only minimal make-up. There was no point in wearing more as she knew she'd cry.

Merida looked gorgeous in a lavender dress and she had taken care of the flowers herself. Purple lilacs for first love, lavender roses for love at first sight, and white heather for protection. 'It also means wishes that come true,' Merida said.

'They're beautiful,' Naomi said, taking her wedding bouquet with shaking hands.

And less than a month after she'd met Abe Devereux, Naomi took the walk to become his wife.

The walk through the hospital was happy one, with smiles and encouragement every step of the way as doctors, patients and relatives alike first stood back to let them pass, and then followed the entourage to steal a peek of this most unexpected wedding.

The music came from a speaker, but was beautiful to all ears as Naomi walked into Jobe's room and saw Abe, standing by his father's bed, smiling *for* her, encouraging her, as he always would.

He wore a charcoal-grey suit, as did Ethan.

Two brothers, who had both known privilege and hell, smiled when the bride arrived, but when he saw she was struggling Abe came over and held out his hand for her to take so he could walk his bride down their makeshift aisle.

It was then Naomi started to cry because, twenty-five years later than most, Naomi found herself loved.

And, thirty-four years later than most, Abe *let* himself be loved.

They kissed before the service.

This backward love they'd found, which was both instant and savoured and would be confirmed at a time of their choosing.

When her nerves had calmed somewhat, he released her from his embrace and walked her to the bedside, and Naomi found another hand waiting to hold hers.

Jobe.

He was in bed but wearing a silk dressing gown,

and pinned to it was a lilac rose. He looked so happy and proud and gave her hand a squeeze.

'You look wonderful,' he told her.

'Thank you,' Naomi said, and squeezed his frail hand back.

'Today,' the officiant said, 'we celebrate the union of Abe and Naomi…' And then she smiled. 'I have to ask if anyone has an objection.'

There were none.

'Who gives this woman to be wedded to this man?'

'I do,' Jobe said in a strong, clear voice that told how much this day meant to him. He gave one more squeeze of her hand, and then let her go to his son and closed his eyes and savoured their vows.

'I will love and protect you,' Abe said, and he meant it with every beat of his heart.

He pushed the ring onto her finger and there could be nothing more valuable to Naomi than that simple band of gold, for she belonged to another at last and in the nicest of ways.

'You may now kiss your bride.'

He cupped her cheeks with his palms and he looked deep into her eyes, and he would not be rushed, for they had waited for this moment, neither having really expected it to arrive.

Bergamot, wood sage, juniper…and another scent she could not decipher yet it would always and for ever be his.

He kissed her lips and it was hard and *just* thorough enough that she could feel its hum on her lips as she sipped champagne.

And they did not dance and make a fuss because today Jobe was tired, and that was okay, he had given enough…

Naomi to Abe.

'Welcome to the family,' he said as she kissed him goodbye.

And as the stand-in father of the bride he had words for Abe. 'Take care of her.'

'Always.'

Cars tooted as they drove past Central Park and love was in the cold air as they approached the hotel.

Abe led her up the very steps that a few nights ago she had run down, crying.

'Mr and Mrs Devereux…' The door was held open and his grip was tight on her hand as they stepped inside.

The foyer was as beautiful as she remembered. More so, for all the roses on the tree had opened and their fragrance was splendid, only this time she didn't linger.

His hand was in the small of her back and she was terribly conscious of it in the most pleasant of ways.

And he remained the perfect gentleman as the elevator carried them to the top floor.

They stepped into the suite and gold drapes were

drawn and the lights were dim and they were finally together, alone.

She was both nervous and shy enough to blush at his seductive gaze but she tried to be bold and reached for him.

'I've got this,' Abe said.

He kissed her then, but not her mouth. He kissed the eyes that had met him at the door on a night when he'd run out of places to hide.

He kissed plump cheeks that blushed so readily and moved to the shell of an ear that had chosen to listen.

Then he kissed slowly down a neck that enticed and he felt the little tremble she gave when her nerves left and the passion they made arrived.

She was shaking, not visibly, but she tremored inside to his skilful caress, and when he slid down her dress and he stood for a moment, just drinking the sight of her in, she knew why she loved him, for with Abe she never had to try and make herself small.

Not physically, they were way past that.

He adored her before he saw her, she knew that.

And she *adored* all she had not seen too.

'I love this,' Naomi said, running her fingers over his flat stomach. His chest she had kissed, and then her hand moved lower.

'Gently,' he warned, when she cupped him too tightly, but they had fun working that out and then he took her to near heaven with his mouth.

'Abe…' she was pleading, but in a way she never had before. He had teased and cajoled with soft, slow sucks and a probing tongue that made deliciously sure she was ready for him.

He moved up her then, kissed her so deeply and weighted her to the bed.

The first nudge of him had her brave, and the second had her unsure.

Her nails dug into his shoulders and Naomi didn't feel so brave now, but this was the first and last time he would willingly hurt her. He could hold back no more and tore in and made her his.

She felt every searing inch and there was no space even to draw breath and scream, as for a second it felt as if the lights went out.

Yet darkness never lasted.

With each slow thrust pain peaked, yet her body welcomed him and he drove in until any discomfort dispersed, building toward an intimacy neither had ever known as she released his shoulders and there was no holding back.

They moved beyond pain, and he thrust in deep, and when he felt her tense beneath him, and the grip and throb of her intimate flesh, only then did he give in.

Abe climbed out of bed and she watched as he moved the champagne bucket by their bed, opened the bottle and poured them both a drink.

'Are you going to kick me out again?' he asked, remembering the last bottle of champagne they'd shared in her room.

'Not this time.' Naomi smiled.

He removed the silver cloche and there was a feast of delicacies to sate both appetites, but before coming back to bed he pulled back the drapes.

'There're lights,' Naomi murmured, still high from their lovemaking, but then she realised there must be a party going on in the park.

'It's New Year's Eve,' Abe reminded her.

'So it is.' Naomi smiled, choosing from the delicacies to eat. But then came the very inappropriate buzz of his phone.

'You are *not* checking your phone on our wedding night,' Naomi warned.

Not that he listened.

Abe had planned this night down to the last detail.

'It's for us,' he told her.

'Us?'

Naomi still wasn't used to hearing that, and frowned when she took his phone.

And he watched as that frown was replaced with a smile.

'It's from Merida and Ethan. Happy New Year, Mr and Mrs Devereux, from your brother-in-law, sister-in-law and your still awake niece.'

And he watched as tears filled in her eyes as another pinged in.

Happy New Year. Dad.

This was family.

There were fireworks lighting up a New York sky and she was in bed with her husband, the person she most loved, but there were others out there, loving them too.

'Happy New Year,' Abe said, and he kissed her tears and he kissed her eyes and he held her close enough to hear his heart.

It truly was.

* * * * *

COMING NEXT MONTH FROM

HARLEQUIN Presents®

Available December 18, 2018

#3681 THE SECRET KEPT FROM THE ITALIAN

Secret Heirs of Billionaires

by Kate Hewitt

Rejected after one mind-blowing night, Maisie kept her pregnancy a secret. Now Antonio's determined to claim his daughter. But their connection reminds Maisie that she still has to protect her heart—because billionaires don't wed waitresses...do they?

#3682 CARRYING THE SHEIKH'S BABY

One Night With Consequences

by Heidi Rice

When shy Cat is hired by Sheikh Zane, she's thrilled—and completely dazzled by their overwhelming chemistry! But their passionate encounter has lasting consequences, and carrying Zane's heir means one thing—Cat must become his queen!

#3683 THE TYCOON'S SHOCK HEIR

by Bella Frances

Restoring his family's legacy is all that's important to Matteo. Yet when Ruby confesses she's pregnant, Matteo demands his child. But with heat still burning between them, can Matteo ignore his desire for Ruby, too?

#3684 THE SPANIARD'S UNTOUCHED BRIDE

Brides of Innocence

by Maisey Yates

Camilla refuses to abandon her beloved horses when Matias acquires her family's *rancho*. Instead, she disguises herself as his stable boy! Yet when Camilla's charade is discovered, Matias offers her an even more shocking role—as his wife!

HPCNM1218RA

#3685 MY BOUGHT VIRGIN WIFE

Conveniently Wed!

by Caitlin Crews

I've never wanted anything like I want Imogen. I married her to secure my empire—but my wife has ignited a hunger in me. I will strip away her obedience, and replace it with a passion to match my own...

#3686 AWAKENING HIS INNOCENT CINDERELLA

by Natalie Anderson

Gracie is mortified when Rafaele finds her accidentally trespassing on his estate! She can't refuse Rafe's teasing demand that she attend an exclusive party with him. Can she resist the power of his raw sensuality?

#3687 CLAIMED FOR THE BILLIONAIRE'S CONVENIENCE

by Melanie Milburne

When headlines mistakenly announce Holly's engagement to Zack, she's stunned. Yet Zack seems determined to turn this scandal, and their red-hot attraction, to their mutual advantage...

#3688 ONE NIGHT WITH THE FORBIDDEN PRINCESS

Monteverro Marriages

by Amanda Cinelli

Facing an arranged marriage, runaway Princess Olivia pleads with billionaire bodyguard Roman to allow her just one week of freedom. But secluded on his private island, their forbidden attraction is explosively undeniable!
